HARD BARGAIN

SHADOW OF THE DOMINION: BOOK 2

BLAZE WARD

KNOTTED ROAD PRESS

Hard Bargain
Shadow of the Dominion: Book 2
Blaze Ward
Copyright © 2019 Blaze Ward
All rights reserved
Published by Knotted Road Press
www.KnottedRoadPress.com

ISBN: 978-1-64470-075-4

Cover art:

ID 73131548 © Algol | Dreamstime.com

Cover and interior design copyright © 2019 Knotted Road Press

Never miss a release!
If you'd like to be notified of new releases, sign up for my
newsletter.

I will never spam you, or use your email for nefarious purposes.
You can also unsubscribe at any time.

http://www.blazeward.com/newsletter/

Shadow of the Dominion

Longshot Hypothesis

Hard Bargain

Outermost

Dominion-427

Phoenix

Princess Rualoh

The Jessica Keller Chronicles

Auberon

Queen of the Pirates

Last of the Immortals

Goddess of War

Flight of the Blackbird

The Red Admiral

St. Legier

Winterhome

CS-405

Queen Anne's Revenge

Packmule

Persephone

Additional Alexandria Station Stories

The Story Road

Siren

Two Bottles of Wine with a War God

The Science Officer Series

The Science Officer

The Mind Field

The Gilded Cage

The Pleasure Dome

The Doomsday Vault

The Last Flagship

The Hammerfield Gambit

The Hammerfield Payoff

Earth Force Sky Patrol

Birth of the Star Dragon

Flight of the Star Dragon

Call of the Star Dragon

Shadow of the Star Dragon

Trial of the Star Dragon

Other Science Fiction Stories

Myrmidons

Moonshot

Menelaus

Earthquake Gun

Moscow Gold

Fairchild

White Crane

The Collective Universe

The Shipwrecked Mermaid

Imposters

[1]
KYRIAKI

IT WAS ODD, as Kyriaki thought about it. She kept a secret that many people would kill for. One of the darkest, most dangerous things possible, anywhere in the galaxy, as far as she knew.

She should have arrested the man. Hauled him back to Cronus Prime in chains, where she would have been celebrated as one of the greatest security officers of all time. But every time she thought about it, Valentinian Tarasicodissa got into her head and muddled everything. And he didn't know the truth about Dave. Only she did.

Knew that Dave had volunteered to go to his death at her command, if she would just let him rescue his captain first. Had even offered gain, after it was done.

Instead, she had helped him rescue his kidnapped captain, and then provided him an escape afterwards, when he was ready to surrender to her and her badge, and go home to be executed as a traitor. And she still didn't really understand why.

She supposed, lying in her warm bed trying to sleep, that it might make her a traitor as well. Certainly, if the truth ever came out, there would be no distance she could run to escape.

Even Dave Hall, the name the man went by now, would be simply shot by his hunters, but Inspector Kyriaki Apokapes, an honored officer of the Dominion's Internal Security forces, would be seen as a worse conspirator.

They would never stop hunting her down if they found out. Even death would only be an escape for her soul, as her comrades would disinter her corpse to haul home and burn, if nothing else.

And she could offer no good excuse for her actions. Lots of bad ones, but that just made her a bad person. Dave Hall wasn't behind any of them, other than as an example of an honorable man.

And then there was the reason she couldn't explain. The man that had caused her to stay her execution. Valentinian.

Nobody would believe that she had felt an instant attraction to Captain Valentinian Tarasicodissa, even before she knew his name. That he just smelled right, in a way unlike anyone else she had ever met. That part of her reason for digging so deep into the man's past in the first place came from a desire to find something she could hate about him. To justify walking away.

And that things only got worse when that hateful thing, whatever it might have been, wasn't there.

Or that she felt like she owed Dave Hall for backing her up at that moment when the bad guys might have gotten away with whatever murder and mayhem they had planned.

She still could have arrested him at the end. The man had actually closed up his telescoping baton sword and been ready to hand it to her, so that she could put him in cuffs and make the arrest of a lifetime.

After he had just killed or disabled at least five men armed with flamer pistols in a small office. A space he had reached by using some sort of parkour technique to bounce off the side of a building and catch a grip on a fire escape five meters in the air with one hand, and then pull himself up so he could climb the rest of the way.

She couldn't do that today, and Dave Hall was nearly twice her age, at least fifty years old, an age when one's physical capabilities had already receded to the point that one must rely on their wits to get by. What must that man have been like when he first ascended the throne?

Good enough to win a Tournament of Domination. Good enough to get himself appointed Supreme Leader of the entire Dominion, and then hold that title for twenty-five years.

Good enough to suffer a secret mid-life crisis. To plan a way to fake his own death and escape the gilded cage he had lived in, and then somehow maneuver a number of highly competent players in such a way that he would have disappeared forever, had Inspector Kyriaki Apokapes, *White Hat* cop, not pressed. Not dug into Tarasicodissa's background and turned her own bosses onto the captain's trail.

Kyriaki gave up sleep and threw back the blanket. She slid across the bed and pulled on a pair of loose, warm pants to go with the shirt she slept in. She was awake, and that wasn't going to change for a while.

She could survive a night with little sleep. Wouldn't be the first. Not likely to be the last, not while she wore the Dominion's White Beret.

Instead, she pulled her pillows up and leaned herself back against the headboard to meditate. Almost as good as sleep, and maybe she would be able to calm all her racing thoughts enough that she could catnap for a while before dawn.

Tomorrow, she would need to give evidence before a grand jury in the case of the Dominion versus Axarnashalic 'Nash' Bogomelous. It was an airtight case. She had arrested the man in the act of kidnapping two Dominion citizens with force and deadly weapons. And she had legitimately deputized Dave Hall to help her, so the six men killed or crippled in the process of getting arrested all got charged with capital murder to go with everything else.

They were all going down, and she would still look like a hero.

Kyriaki was already prepared to seem extremely surprised and disappointed when Valentinian and Dave failed to show up at the hearing, but their absence would not impact the case. Lianearia Cleray was no longer chartering Valentinian's ship, the *Longshot Hypothesis*, and had remained behind on Tartarus while her troupe put on performances and the woman sought alternate transport.

A former business partner of Bogomelous, she would be all too happy to see that man prosecuted, right after he got out of the hospital from the wound Dave had inflicted on him with a blunt sword. The kind that had permanently shattered the man's knee cap, when she knew Hall was good enough to have severed his shin instead. Hall hadn't missed with his swing.

No, Dave and Valentinian would officially disappear. Gone, just like that. She had warned both of them to do exactly that before calling in the local Security detachment to arrest everyone.

And they had.

She believed Dave Hall that Valentinian didn't know the truth, but could still be relied upon to flee at the first opportunity. And she would cover for both of them as long as she could, for reasons she could barely explain to herself.

A chime on her nightstand caused Kyriaki's eyes to open, her meditative state shattering like a dropped glass. That tone was reserved for the security band, and nobody on this planet knew to get a hold of her that way.

She leaned over and grabbed the card-reader, checking the sender. Ambassador Rodosthenis Mataraci. Her boss's boss back home. The head of the White Hats on Dominion Prime, the Dominator's Winter Palace station in orbit of Cronus Prime, the capital itself.

Here.

Have arrived with news. Urgent we meet soonest. Send location and ETA. RM

Well, that was one way to completely ruin her evening. Nothing like possibly getting your hand caught in the cookie jar at the very moment you were apparently suffering a crisis of conscience.

It was a good thing Valentinian and Dave had a good head start.

Their time had just run out.

Hopefully, not hers as well.

VALENTINIAN

IT WAS a thing of utter beauty to Valentinian. A rarity in a hand of poker that was almost unbeatable, but he had to be careful not to spook his fish by betting too heavy, too quickly.

He scowled at his cards, like he was going to try to bluff a High Stack/Low Stack, rather than the Mixed Pyramid he had drawn with his sixth card. It was a four color mess: Crowns, Trophies, Swords, and Coins, but the only real way someone would beat him right now was to pull their own Perfect Pyramid, and he only ever seen that happen twice in his life.

For the nigglingest moment, he wondered if the four people at the table with him had somehow managed to stack the deck, to get him all in right now, where they could clean him out, but that wouldn't be that much money. Valentinian was too cheap to ever play poker with people for more than a few hundred Solars. Or, since he was now in Laurentian space, aboard Bohrne Station, the currency was Union Krodageni. The conversion wasn't an exact science, but the twenty-five hundred or so in front of him came out to about five hundred Solars, after he paid arbitrage fees to the bank to convert them for him.

Certainly not enough to warrant even a high-powered game, and this looked to be pretty small potatoes, even for a shithole in the middle of nowhere like this space station.

Valentinian had only gotten into the game out of boredom, more than anything. And to keep his card skills sharp. He had originally won the stake that bought his Anuradhan cargo transport, *Longshot Hypothesis*, in a much more rigged game, three years ago, when the big players had set up a deep-pockets mark and let Valentinian quietly rake off a couple of nice pots towards the end as camouflage for their impending sledgehammer on the sucker.

Look around the table. If you can't spot the mark, it's you.

Valentinian was pretty sure two or maybe three of the other players were marks for the old guy who had been at the table the longest.

Valentinian studied the man across the table. They weren't in the classic back room, but this was at least a quiet, well-lit corner in a reasonably laidback bar, on a backwoods station on the far side of Laurentia, well away from the Dominion. Not the end of the civilized universe, but you could smell it from here. Hit warpspace and run hard and you'd be there in two weeks.

The old man smiled at Valentinian with his eyes and nothing else. Like he had somehow marked the cards ahead of time and knew what Valentinian held in his hand. And had checked the bid on a High Stack of Shields showing, deferring to the big kid on Valentinian's left who had more money than sense, the one with maybe a whiff of desperation.

And a tendency towards verbal abuse of people perhaps a shade out of line for total strangers met in a bar.

But the kid was big. And probably thought that size meant something. Like maybe Valentinian wouldn't just shoot him with a shock pistol or hit him with a chair in a bar fight. To say nothing of the old man. Valentinian knew better than to start shit with that one, just from the way he held his eyes.

And he didn't need to, with the one, big dude at the bar, dressed like a common spacer off a freight transport and watching the game with a vaguely interested eye. Plus a telescoping baton tucked into a pocket that Valentinian had seen Dave use in close combat to kill people so fast they died on their feet first and then fell over.

The kid dropped a hundred Union Krodageni into the pot and thrust out his jaw smugly, like maybe he could buy everyone else into folding their strong hands and letting him rake it with a weak one. The old man's behavior made a lot more sense if he didn't like the kid, and had the skill to stack the deck on a shuffle.

Yet another reason Valentinian never gambled with money he didn't want to lose at the table. This was just for entertainment tonight, because he had wanted to be around people for a few hours.

But sure, he could play.

Valentinian made a performance of checking his

cards again, like he was trying to do some fancy mathing in his head without giving away too much.

"Bid's one hundred to you, punk," the kid said roughly.

Valentinian fixed the man with a blank, owl stare. It was rude to think of him as a kid, since he was probably a few years older than Valentinian's twenty-three, but he had all the polish and sophistication of a sixteen-year-old on his first trip away from home.

The old man smiled, again only with his eyes.

"Huh," Valentinian decided to play along. He could lose three quarters of the chips in front of him right now and still break even tonight. These people were amateurs. Plus there was all the entertainment he'd had playing, which was its own value. "Guess I'll meet that. No, let's raise it eighteen."

It sounded like an annoying number. Right now, he was more interested in irritating the kid than cleaning out the two folks on the right. Wouldn't stop him, mind you, but they might only be considered collateral damage, and not the primary target.

"Eighteen?" the kid rasped. "What the hell?"

Nearest person on his right folded, but Valentinian wasn't surprised. He was pretty sure that the person was a she, but it was hard to tell, as they were muffled to the eyeballs in a warm coat, scarf, fingerless gloves, and a knit cap. And it was already warm enough in here that Valentinian was reconsidering wearing his black jacket, the light shell he wore most places because he kept his ship a few degrees cooler than anyone else did.

Any way to save a few Solars on his fuel bill.

That triggered the other player to fold, too, leaving just the old man.

"Call," the man drawled. "No, tell you what. Raise you eleven."

"What the hell is wrong with you people?" the kid growled louder than was politely necessary for folks less than a table away.

"I believe the call is twenty-nine?" Valentinian let his voice get supercilious at the punk. Just because.

"Fifty," the punk grabbed five coins and flung them almost across the table.

The person in the cold weather gear shoved two runaways back into the middle.

"Twenty-two to me?" Valentinian asked absently.

"I believe thirty-two," the old man responded in the sort of tone that suggested afternoon tea instead of evening poker.

"Oh, yes. Of course," Valentinian said. "How silly of me."

He made a performance out of counting out thirty-two coins, counting them again, and then counting them a third time just because, before carefully adding them to the pile, just to watch steam emerge from the kid's ears in frustration.

"Fold," the old man suddenly turned his cards over and leaned back with the faintest hint of a wink on the side of his face the kid wouldn't see.

Huh. So it was a set-up.

What did you do to piss off that old man, punk?

Old guy was still the dealer, so the seventh cards went out. Face down. The Build card from which you were supposed to erect a perfect pyramid. If you could.

The punk's eyes flashed with anger for the briefest instant, like he had missed drawing the card he needed and was hoping four of a kind would be enough.

Might be, in some games. With people who didn't loathe you. Or old men who could stack decks as adroitly as this one apparently had.

It would be the last hand, that was for certain. Valentinian wasn't going to play for these stakes with a card sharp. Old man probably realized that, and had decided to take the punk down a peg in the process.

Looking at his Build card, Valentinian had the second Capstone of Crowns, so it was almost mathematically impossible that a better hand could exist on the table. And certainly not with the three Wedgestones the kid was showing.

Valentinian watched the kid start to push his whole stack forward.

"All in," he growled, looking at Valentinian with an angry dare in his eyes.

"Count it," Valentinian challenged. "I've got more chips than you do."

Serious grumbling. Angry words that stayed just enough under the breath that Valentinian could pretend he didn't hear them if he wanted to.

The old man's right hand had strayed off the table, almost absently. Valentinian didn't figure the guy would come up shooting, and Dave was close enough that the big guy could do something if he did, but that hand might come back up with a pistol, if the kid got out of hand.

Which smelled kinda likely right now.

"Seven hundred and fifty-eight Union

Krodageni," the kid snarled in a voice only barely human.

Valentinian barely glanced at the kid, watching the old man's eyes, but the man didn't move. Perhaps nodded just a hint.

Valentinian counted out chips. Seven hundred and fifty eight was a tiny amount right now, maybe a quarter of what was in front of him. He pushed it forward a little with a cold smile. Then he picked up a chip and tossed it in as well.

"Raise you one," Valentinian said quietly.

"That's all I got," the kid snarled.

"Pity," Valentinian said in a voice like death. "Guess you're out, then. Unless you have something that maybe is worth an extra Krodageni. Rules say table stakes only, but since it's just you and me right now, I'm willing to stretch them, just a bit. This once, mind you."

The kid thought about it for a few seconds and then stabbed a hand inside his jacket so quickly that the old man's pistol was up and centered on his face before anybody at the table could blink.

"Bring it out really slowly, son," the old man drawled.

The other two players were probably puckered up pretty hard right now, but neither of them had moved.

Kid turned white. Valentinian was pretty sure he'd only ever seen one man move that fast. Fortunately, Dave Hall just happened to be watching from the old man's blind spot.

If the old man actually had one.

Slowly, oh so slowly, the kid grabbed something with two fingers and pulled it clear of the pocket inside his jacket. It was a piece of plas-paper, triple-folded inward and held with a tab.

"What is that?" the old man asked in a dry tone.

"A treasure map," the kid offered.

That might be the first honest thing he had said all day. Absolutely the most polite.

"Worth a cred?" the old man asked Valentinian.

"I'll allow it," Valentinian decided.

What the hell. It would be a doozy of a story, if nothing else. How many people could honestly say they had won a treasure map in a crooked card game, after all?

The map went onto the pile, somewhere north of four thousand Union Krodageni at this point.

The kid turned over five of a kind, all Wedgestones. His face just about collapsed when Valentinian turned over a Mixed Pyramid. His breath escaped like a burst balloon.

Suddenly he stood up in a terrible rage.

"You bastards cheated me," he screamed at the top of his lungs. "I oughta kill the lot of you!"

Which was pretty impressive, considering the old man still had a pistol in his hand. Before the kid could move, the old man flicked back the lapel of his jacket with his off hand to reveal a big, silver star of a badge, literally pinned to his shirt.

"You took all my money!" the kid raged, but carefully never moved forward that one step that would get him shot. "What the hell do I do now?"

"For one, you stop threatening random people on my station with violence," the old man's drawl went hot. "I don't like people like you, and I've had reports these last few days, but nothing worth doing something about you until now. Do you understand me?"

Now the kid was white. Probably never had actual consequences catch up with him before. He looked like a farm boy. Dave's size, but a couple of extra layers of fat over the muscle, and probably no real danger to anything but females.

And he looked like the type that hit girls.

"Sheriff, if I may?" Valentinian offered quietly.

The old man glanced over.

Valentinian pulled two hundred Union Krodageni off the pot, setting them into two stacks of ten coins.

"Kid, here's one hundred to cover your food and sundries," Valentinian said. "Sheriff, will one hundred get him on a transport to somebody else's station?"

"It would," the old man allowed. "You sure?"

"I am," Valentinian said.

It had been a setup, but obviously so that the sheriff could get a bully trapped in a bad place honestly. Maybe not one hundred percent legal, but a nice, ethical solution. Valentinian liked the way the old man worked.

"You willing to walk away, kid?" the old man asked.

"What about my map?" he cried, suddenly a little forlorn.

"I'm keeping the map, kid," Valentinian said. "Go home before someone like one of us decides to take your soul instead of settling for all your money."

That fully deflated the kid. Took away that last pillar of anger that had been holding him up. He slumped.

Valentinian really appreciated the way the sheriff

nodded to a pair of spacers sitting in a far corner, who both stood up, took off their jackets, and suddenly turned into deputies.

Pretty sneaky trick.

"Take this and buy him passage on the shuttle to Pannotia," the sheriff instructed the deputies as they took the kid into hand and gathered up the coins.

Valentinian made sure that the kid got his other coins as well. It could be a long, nasty ride in the dark, on some ships, if you could barely afford to eat. One hundred Union Krodageni would keep him in food for a month, if he was careful. Valentinian had been forced to do it the hard way a few times. He wouldn't begrudge the kid a few hot meals.

"Thank you," the sheriff's gun was gone and there was a bright smile on his face as he turned back to the table. "Figured it was worth an evening to see how bad the kid was, and the risk to my station."

"Blowhard," Valentinian decided. "All hat and no cattle."

"Maybe," the old man agreed. "But all that size is a special kind of trouble, even with your big friend back there keeping watch on us."

Valentinian grinned. He had thought that maybe nobody had noticed Dave. Hadn't expected a sting operation.

And now he was nearly thirty-five hundred Union Krodageni long. Not a bad way to spend a night.

"So what are you doing with the map?" voice on his right broke in.

Valentinian had forgotten about the other two marks in this game. He looked at the one all bundled up, like it was below freezing in here, instead of a pleasant twenty-three warm degrees.

"Hmmm?" Valentinian studied…her? Voice sounded kinda like a her. No clue what they might look like, since there were so many layers built up on top.

"The map?" they repeated earnestly.

Valentinian picked it up and opened it. Sets of numbers down the right looked like nav coordinates and vectors. Center was a two-dimensional representation of the three-dimensional space. No place Valentinian recognized off the top of his head, but he was also clear onto the far side of Laurentia right now. Wildspace was not all that far away, if he kept on his previous course of running like hell to get away from the Dominion.

The sheriff took a quick look when Valentinian laid it flat, but just grunted and stood.

"Not anything I need to worry about," he announced happily, departing.

The other player departed as well, leaving Valentinian with the person seated on his right.

"Buy it for a credit," the person announced.

"Nope," Valentinian decided. "Keeping it. Hell of a trophy. Why do you want it?"

"That looks like a salvager's map," they said, pointing with a dark fingertip. "See these symbols? Looks like an old ship of some kind has been parked somewhere, and someone thought it was valuable enough to make a map like this to be able to get back to it at a later date."

"What do you know about salvage?" Valentinian was surprised. They hadn't spoken much during the game, mostly because of the abuse that would erupt from the kid whenever they did.

Valentinian noted Dave standing and moving over with a plastic cup of the house beer, the weak stuff, before the big man took the chair the sheriff had played from.

"I'm a salvager," they announced, sticking out a hand. "Bayjy Endon."

Valentinian shook the hand. Gender was still iffy, but the hands had done serious work in an armored space suit at some point, that much was clear from the callouses he could feel.

They pulled the hood back a little and the scarf down enough to show off a hairless face that looked female as well. Except that her skin was a soft purple somewhere between orchid and mauve, instead of the brownish hues of he and Dave.

She had black eyeballs, with reddish irises, but she grinned and looked friendly enough.

"Valentinian Tarasicodissa," he said, and then pointed. "Dave Hall, my first mate. Any idea where this map might center?"

"None," Bayjy said. "But if you wanna go look, then I'm your gal."

"I'm pretty sure I've never met your kind, Bayjy ," Valentinian offered, trying to be polite and careful, while dealing with a purple woman. "Where are you from?"

"Oh, I'm Pranai," she scoffed. "You two aren't from around here, are you?"

"Nope," Valentinian agreed with her. "Just got this far out, but originally from deep in the Dominion."

"Really?" she was surprised. "Wow. You are a

LOOONNNGG ways from home, cowboy. What brings you?"

"Salvage, apparently," Valentinian grinned at the woman. "Can I buy you a drink?"

"Buy me dinner," she countered. "All this gambling works up a hunger, and I'm burning calories furiously, just trying to stay warm in this icebox."

"What's your homeworld like?" Dave asked politely.

"Thirty-two on a cold day," Bayjy smiled at the big man and laughed. "I like it around forty-five. How you weirdoes survive barely above freezing astounds me."

Valentinian laughed with her. They had only stopped here to take on supplies and look for cargo that needed to be hauled.

Maybe he needed to go looking for buried treasure, too.

THE LOCAL TIME of night was about an hour after the dance halls had closed up and kicked everybody out, so the all-night restaurant was pretty full, but most of the people here were in small groups intent on coming down from a physical high so they could get a few hours of sleep and then head back into the factory or the office after the sun rose.

Kyriaki didn't exactly fit in, but she also didn't stand out, other than being dressed in a set of pants and a jacket in browns, where everybody else wore the brightest, sparklingest stuff they owned. They even sounded like peacocks screeching at each other, but she could ignore them, once the waitress delivered a mug of coffee.

Might as well assume no sleep, and catnap tomorrow as needed. The Ambassador was on Dominion Prime time right now, not the local clock, and if he had come here himself, it must be bad.

She watched the man enter the restaurant and look around. Like her, he was dressed in a mufti so anonymous as to be a disguise. On the other hand, while the blond woman with him was dressed as Kyriaki was, in pants and a jacket, she would have stood out on the dance floor of any club on this planet.

The Ambassador was tall and gaunt, bald with lines permanently etched into his skull. The stranger was perhaps a decade younger than the Ambassador, but Kyriaki only had her walk to determine that. She had those genes that made it impossible to tell if a woman was thirty or sixty, if she kept up a good regime in hair dye, like this one apparently had.

The hair was faded gold, if that was a color. Pulled back into a complex braid that still went at least to her shoulder blades. Wasp shape in build, with broad shoulders, a pinched-in waist, and strong hips.

Classically beautiful, if you were to cast her in white marble, but her face was cold and shrewish as they approached. Something about her screamed power, so Kyriaki just assumed the woman was a representative of the Dominion Household. Or an assassin they had sent.

How the hell had they already found out the truth about Dave Hall? She couldn't think of any other reason for those two people to be standing on this planet. And that meant trouble.

Fortunately, everyone was undercover, so she didn't have to rise and bow to honor the woman. The Ambassador, her skip-boss, wasn't necessarily into that level of decorum, except during public rituals where others might note an unacceptable level of informality among his staff, but her and her peers all respected the man immensely. She sat and waited as they saw her, approached, and sat.

She did note that the Ambassador put the woman on the inside of the booth, trapping her against the wall, while Kyriaki had her side to herself.

He paused to study the rest of the room with a harsh eye. The waitress was a little overloaded right now, but friendly, so it would be some minutes before she got to the newcomers. Other tables were getting food delivered as fast as the kitchen could churn it out.

"Inspector Apokapes," the Ambassador nodded and spoke in a quiet, personal voice. "Kyriaki. We are in public, so first names only. You will call me Rodosthenis, or Rod, for now. This woman is Athanasia."

"Rod," Kyriaki nodded back, somewhat aghast at being on a first name basis with the man, even in disguise. "Athanasia."

"You have a very big gold star next to your name, Inspector," Rod grinned at her. "Your interest in pursuing that slenderest of impossible threads caught the attention of elements in the Household, who then reviewed your findings. There are bits of information that even Internal Security is not privy to, as a check on our immense power, but those watchers had all the cards laid out in front of them on the table."

"Ambassador?" Kyriaki let her voice grow concerned and confused.

Hopefully it would be enough to confuse them now. Back home, she knew that they had found Dave Hall finally. Kyriaki couldn't think of anything else. She was just elated that Valentinian had already launched and made it to warpspace before these people ever arrived. The whole planet would be trapped in a lockdown if they hadn't. And then the Dominion Armada would come into play.

Kyriaki watched the woman reach into her jacket and pull out a card. No, a photo on plas-paper, about the size of her palm.

"Do you recognize this man?" she asked peremptorily, resting it on the table.

Athanasia might have had a pleasant voice, but Kyriaki suspected she would have to become a pleasant person first. And Kyriaki didn't see that happening.

Kyriaki looked down at the card. Studied the face. It was close, but not all that close. Could have even been his brother, rather than the fugitive, but this part of the game was up. That much was obvious. Had been since her card-reader chirped an hour ago.

She had an icy tightrope to walk in a high wind, especially with these two people here.

"It looks somewhat like Dave Hall," Kyriaki said carefully. "A bad picture of him, perhaps. Almost different enough to be a sibling or close cousin, instead."

The woman surprised her, and everybody else, by slamming her open palm down on the table top with a resounding snap that reminded Kyriaki of the apocalypse descending.

Athanasia had the courtesy to blush at the sudden disruption as the waitress had just come up to take their order. The woman quietly ordered coffee to get the waitress to depart. Then she looked at the Ambassador mutely.

Staring daggers at someone as a verbal description

had never made sense to Kyriaki, until now. She was just glad the woman was focused on her boss, and not her.

"You are sure?" the Ambassador asked Kyriaki in a calm, careful voice.

"No," Kyriaki said deliberately. If nothing else, the White Hats were never sure of anything. They had levels of confidence. And he knew that. "It appears to be a morphologically similar male of approximately the right age and ethnicity. The eyes are similar. But it feels different from the man I remember from the operation the day before yesterday. I would need to have the man sitting here to identify the exact differences. However, Dave Hall could have used this as an older identity card, and most places would have accepted it."

The Ambassador nodded, like she had earned a point. Another point.

Just because she was lying to protect her own life, as well as Valentinian and Dave, didn't mean she was going to do a half-assed job of it. She still had her professional standards.

"Tell me about the operation," Athanasia asked, her voice growing less shrill, even if it wasn't anywhere close to warm or friendly yet. "I have only read a summary of your report."

"The crew of *Longshot Hypothesis* was hired to transport Solaria Femina as a charter between worlds, starting at Dominion Prime," Kyriaki fell back on the notes in her head. "A former partner of the head of the organization was upset that his contracts had been terminated by the woman in charge, Lianearia Cleray, and chose to kidnap her and the captain of the ship at gun point, two nights ago. I presume some level of psychological or perhaps physical torture was intended, in order to get them to void the existing contracts and sign new ones. There is a preliminary hearing for evidence to keep the prisoners scheduled for later today where I will give testimony."

She paused while they absorbed the background.

"Given that time was critical, and the local authorities perhaps not as trustworthy as they should have been, I deputized Dave Hall on the scene and he assisted me," Kyriaki said. This was all absolute truth, and wouldn't change, even if they put her completely under and subjected her to truth serum. It was only the rest of the story that would get her killed. "I sent Hall up the fire escape while I penetrated the building directly. Kicking in the door, as it were, I took out one, partially disabled a second, and pinned the remainder down enough that Dave was able to catch them by surprise."

"Where he crippled two and killed three more," Athanasia said simply. "With a metal club."

"He moves exceptionally quietly," Kyriaki nodded to the woman. "Plus there was a firefight going on at the front of the suite, so all eyes were on me. As intended. I didn't see his attack. Only the outcome. But there was a reason I brought him and not the local Gendarmes. The man's a killer, and was willing to take my orders in order to rescue his captain."

The Ambassador turned to Athanasia with a questioning look. After a moment, the woman nodded, letting her eyes fall as her head tilted forward, like it had suddenly grown too heavy to hold up.

"Inspector, what I am about to tell you is a secret classified so highly that even I am only allowed to know the truth because it was necessary to pursue this investigation," he said quietly, pausing as the waitress came by to deliver and top off coffee. "You are to be read in now because you have been following this investigation and have all the facts on the ground. Plus, I share your opinion of the local office, but now is not the time to clean it up, and this is absolutely not the case to make a stink about."

"Okay?" Kyriaki replied carefully, like she was holding a sleeping skunk.

To be *read in* was a bureaucratic term that meant that you could now know things that normally were none of your business. *Need To Know.* And apparently they had decided she needed to.

"The public reports will continue to state that the Dominator was assassinated," the Ambassador murmured.

"Dave Hall was the assassin?" she whispered fiercely.

Kyriaki figured it sounded like a good guess here. And the sort of logical conclusion an Inspector might jump to. She even put anger and shock in her voice while keeping the tones inside this booth.

"It is much worse than that, Kyriaki," the man said.

"Sir?" she asked, willing to play this role as long as she could. There were far worse things they could do to her besides just shooting her like a rabid animal.

Rather than speak, he turned to Athanasia, nodding to indicate she should complete the story.

"Dave Hall is not the assassin, Kyriaki," Athanasia said simply. "He is the Dominator."

"The WHAT?" she let her voice rise before she could smother it, but that was the shock that anybody, ANYWHERE, would EVER admit that sort of thing in public.

She had been expecting them to come to her with some cover story, however thin and unbelievable, and get her help sending assassins after Dave and Valentinian. Not that she expected anybody could ever catch *Longshot Hypothesis*, not now if Valentinian suspected the entire Dominion Armada was coming for him.

And they apparently were.

The Ambassador reached out a hand and placed it flat atop the table, which was a way of almost offering her a hand on her arm as comfort. That shocked her even more. She had never suspected the man of having that level of human empathy.

The White Hats were the Dominion's Internal Security troops. They didn't do *Nice*.

"We believe that the man known as the Dominator faked his own death," the Ambassador said quietly. "That he took on the identity of Dave Hall when he set up his escape, and used Valentinian Tarasicodissa and Lianearia Cleray as distractions to keep us confused because they each had their own skeletons in closets. But for your stubborn insistence that something was wrong, we would have been years uncovering the truth. And likely never caught up with the man."

Kyriaki leaned back and let the shock color her body language. Let them think she was surprised at the turn of events. She could use that to her advantage, when she was really amazed that something like this would ever be discussed in public, in a restaurant, no less.

Especially with a low-level officer like her.

"That picture?" Kyriaki asked, nodding without pointing.

"Another identity he used in the middle," Athanasia admitted. "Close enough, as you surmised, to work for the average inspection, but different enough that we did not make the connection when we first looked. It was only when I reviewed your file that I understood that he had become Dave Hall to escape us. From there, it took us several steps backwards to locate the man's starting point."

Us? Oh, shit, this woman was inside the Household itself in some official capacity? Not just a high official of the Solar Party, but at the very top?

Kyriaki didn't even bother trying to calm her racing heartbeat. She wondered if she was about to be executed as a failure to stop the two men. Shooting the messenger wasn't always a figure of speech.

But the cop in her also surged to the fore. That was who she was, so trying to stop it would be like trying to stop breathing.

"No offense, Athanasia, but how can we be sure?" Kyriaki asked both of them sharply.

She was well within her rights and responsibilities to question everyone and everything. That's who the White Hats were.

"Because I knew Dave Hall, when he wore another name," Athanasia replied in a complicated tone.

Kyriaki had expected anger. Or sadness. Something other than *matter-of-fact*.

Kyriaki stared at the woman, waiting for that other shoe to drop. It wasn't going to be pleasant.

"He was my husband," Athanasia said.

[4]
DAVE

IT TURNED out he was getting pretty good at being Dave Hall. Still felt a little off at times. He found himself occasionally having to stop and check himself for tendencies of…that other person.

Dave had taken to calling that man *Yesterday*, so that he didn't even stop to think about a name. And he could talk about yesterday as a place far away, rather than the person who used to inhabit this skin.

And skin had him thinking.

She had light purple skin. Somewhere darker than lavender, but not much. Dave had never met one of the so-called Variant Humanities that populated places like Wildspace and the *Unknown Regions* beyond.

He supposed that *Unknown* was a relative term. People out here probably thought of the Dominion as a distant, magical land, rather than the center of the known universe.

To each her own.

Valentinian was in a rather cheerful mood as they

sat at the table and chatted. Dave put that down to being able to spring for a huge, expensive dinner on someone else's cash, considering the money that the sheriff had raked off the bully before arresting him. Normally, they would eat simple fare on the ship, or occasionally wander out to the station for cheap eats, but the sheriff had called a nice steakhouse and made them reservations, even though he wouldn't be joining them.

The private room they found themselves in wasn't petite, but it wasn't the sort of grand hall Dave had known in the old days. Where entertaining fifty people, all wearing half-masks to hide their faces, was normal.

It was still bizarre to eat with strangers, with a naked face, but Dave knew, at least intellectually, that most of the galaxy did it that way.

Weirdoes.

Still, Dave Hall could adapt.

And the restaurant was adapting as well. The three of them were in a private room, with the heat turned up to maybe thirty-five degrees. Enough that Valentinian was wearing only his white shirt, and Dave had stripped down to his undertunic, with his main tunic slung over a side chair.

Bayjy, on the other hand, was down to just a sweatshirt right now, advertising for some university sports team Dave didn't know. And her knit cap. The gloves had come off, but she kept her hands wrapped around an oversized coffee mug to keep them warm.

She had a lively smile. The face looked vaguely demonic when he studied her, but that was a number of little things, rather than one big item. She had no hair on her head, other than eyelashes and the faintest wisps of eyebrows. Nor any on the backs of her hands, as near as he could tell without actually touching her.

The bones in her face were heavy, for lack of a better term. From what he had seen as she stripped off her parka, she might outweigh him, but it looked to be all muscle and bone, with her being at least as broad across the shoulders as him, and just barely taller than Valentinian, depending on the shoes she was wearing.

Scarred hands gave proof of hard work with heavy equipment. Caelon armor left similar marks, but hers looked like they came from a powered liftersuit. The kind you used to salvage wrecks, apparently.

At least that was her story.

They all had stories to tell. Some of them might even be the truth, depending on how you wanted to shade it and what details you chose to exclude to protect the guilty. He had escaped a bad marriage and a mid-life crisis to go off and see the galaxy.

More or less.

And Valentinian was just a merchant captain trying to make enough Solars to stay ahead of maintenance and repairs, while putting money away to retire someday.

"So if your people aren't from anywhere near here, how did you end up in Laurentia?" Valentinian was asking Bayjy.

He and Dave were drinking chilled soda water with coconut cream and pineapple juice, two tropical exports of the planet below them. And lots of ice. All the hot coffee was going into the woman with them to keep her teeth from chattering.

Dave noted the scowl that passed across the woman's face. Like she had thought too much about this story and not found any good answers, but knew it would come up and she'd have to come clean. More or less.

"We got dumped here," she growled, teeth clenched so hard her jaw muscles stuck out.

"Dumped?" Dave asked in a slow tone.

"My last captain had told us that he could get a much better price for our last cargo here in Laurentia, than at some of the other fences he knew, deeper in Wildspace," she muttered through clenched teeth.

"What happened?" Valentinian asked after she dropped silent for a long stretch.

Bayjy sighed, a mix of anger and resignation.

"Bastard docked and gave us all twenty-seven hours station leave as a reward for busting our asses on that last derelict," she shrugged. "Once we were all clear and inside drinking, he undocked and disappeared."

Dave liked the sort of violence that came into Valentinian's eyes at those words. One of the reasons he had chosen the man when making his own escape had been that odd mixture of ethics and criminality the records showed. A good man, badly used, but not letting it turn him into a bad man.

"This ship got a name?" Valentinian asked in a voice that didn't even hint at casual curiosity.

"*Hard Bargain*," Bayjy's tone matched his captain. "Captain's Butler Vidy-Wooders, but you should probably stay away from the man."

"Why's that?" Dave asked in his own bright, curious tone.

"Butler's a M'Rai," Bayjy said, staring at him.

Almost daring him to say something before she shook her head. "No? Nothing? Huh, you two *are* lost. M'Rai are nearly three meters tall. At least Butler is. Another of the so-called Variant Humanities you find out here."

"Why are they called Variants?" Valentinian asked. "And let's just presume I'm farther from home than I've ever been, okay?"

"Huh? Oh, right," she said, pausing to suck down some coffee and then refill her mug from the carafe the waitress had delivered when they ordered steaks.

"So once upon a time," she began, pausing to chuckle wickedly. "I never got to actually say that before, so it's kinda cool and you'll just have to deal with it. One upon a time there was this big empire, more or less centered on what is Wildspace today. The Urlan's ancestors had conquered all of it and had a bunch of subject species, but humans bred the fastest of all so those folks decided to experiment on us. Pranai, T'Brask, M'Rai. Bunch of others. All redesigned for some specific environment or need. Then the humans, all the Variants included, revolted, with the help of some other folk, like the Sh'Vaadig. War lasted a couple thousand years, I guess, and when it was done, the Urlan Empire had been destroyed, and a whole bunch of planets with it."

"Destroyed?" Valentinian perked up and Dave leaned closer. "How?"

"Big rocks," she said. "Dirty Nukes. Bio-weapons. Couple of robot armies dropped on surfaces with xenocide orders baked in. Nasty stuff. Everything went to hell. Only been the last thousand years or so that people started really getting organized again. Mostly it had been lone planets or small groups. And lots of Wildspace is still a little too radioactive to really colonize some of the planets, but there's a ton of old gear floating around in space. Metal's generally not worth anything, but some of them are armed, or have some useful gear you can strip or loot. That's where we came in."

"And your captain got greedy and decided to cut you all out of your shares?" Valentinian asked in a cold, lethal tone that made even Dave double-take. "That about it?"

Dave wasn't sure he'd ever seen Vee this angry. Made him feel warm and fuzzy inside.

Apparently, Bayjy saw the same thing, because her smile returned. Dave suspected it might be irrepressible, but she had gotten dark there. And with good reason.

"That's about it," she agreed. "Everyone else split and tried to get back to places they knew on their own, further out, but I wanted to see where the hell I ended up. Heard stories about the boring zones, figured I should see them with my own eyes."

"Boring zones?" Dave asked.

"Hey, I grew up on the fringes of Wildspace, Dave," she grinned. "This place is a backwater, as far as I'm concerned."

"You any good?" Valentinian asked. "As a salvager?"

"I'm the best there is, Valentinian," she snapped back with a snark in her tone. "And I'm pretty good as a salvager, too."

"I see," Valentinian nodded and let it drop with the faintest grin.

"Don't you worry," Bayjy said. "Boys like you'd probably be too fragile for a woman like me."

"Hadn't really offered," Valentinian offered dryly.

"Oh, I understand," Bayjy smiled. "But you get on a ship for a few months, and sometimes some of the boys get a little needy, and think they can just take something, rather than asking. Not opposed to someone asking nice, but figured I'd get that out on the table up front."

"Understood," Valentinian agreed. "More interested in salvaging as an art form."

"Good choice of words," Bayjy said. "Any fool can cut a ship up, but there's an art and a science to finding the good stuff, and making the fewest possible cuts necessary in order to get your treasure out. Anything else and you waste too much time, or haul too much worthless metal back to the fence to sell. Neither's profitable."

"So what did *Hard Bargain* find?" Dave asked, trying to keep them from losing the bit of the story that had interested him.

He could see both of them on the verge of nerding out over salvage. He didn't think Vee had ever done something like that, at least not from the records Dave had seen, but free money floating in space, just waiting for someone to come get it, was the sort of thing Valentinian would perk up at. Like dogs and bones.

Bayjy fixed him with a hard look. Like maybe studying him as a person, finally, and not just hired muscle. He was also that, but he had learned a few things in the process of running a major interstellar empire for more than two decades.

"It was an old Urlan troopship," she said after a few moments of *considering*. "Not a lot of tech, but there was a chapel and a bunch of old religious relics and paraphernalia we were able to grab. I figure Butler's greed overcame his specism on the Urlan and he decided to go find one of their worlds so he could sell all this stuff directly, without giving a fence a cut, or us."

"Hopefully we'll run into the guy, one of these days," Dave smiled. "And I can convey your greetings to the man properly."

"He's got nearly a meter on you, Dave," she said carefully.

"Yes," Dave agreed. "That might make it a fair fight for him. Maybe not. Maybe I'll let him bring some friends."

"Is he that crazy or that dangerous?" she turned her attention to Valentinian.

"Or?" Vee grinned. "Both."

"Good to know," she announced with her own grin. "So how do I convince you to hire an expert?"

"Still not sure I'm going after the thing," Valentinian replied. "Got out here looking for cargo jobs, because I got bills that don't stop just because I spend my evenings playing poker and entertaining pretty ladies."

Dave liked the grin that came across Bayjy's face. Irrepressible. Much better than the scowl she had held before. And maybe he would find this Butler fellow at some point.

People like that needed to have their asses kicked occasionally. And Vee certainly wouldn't mind helping.

"Well until then, you two are babes in the woods out here," she said matter-of-factly. "So you can hire me as a tour guide for now. That gives us time to build up the right kind of equipment for salvaging, when that treasure map finally starts whispering in your ear as you try to sleep."

"Hard sell?" Valentinian asked.

"Hey, I just watched you play poker for nearly three hours," Bayjy replied tartly. "You can learn a lot about a person that way. And I have nothing better to do right now but try to hustle up my next gig. Not broke, but not exactly rolling in the cash, either. Tell me about your ship. He fast?"

Valentinian kind of cocked his head at the woman, but Dave appreciated her forthrightness. It was a welcome change from a world of masks and hidden identities.

"Yeah, fast enough," Valentinian said in an offhand way.

"So nothing in the galaxy can probably keep up with you but priority military transports?" she asked with a warm chuckle. "I know how you spacers are when you get subtle."

"Maybe a few others, on a good day," Valentinian shrugged. "High end of tonnage for a light cargo transport, plus six cabins for paying passengers. Recently was hauling eighteen people, but they were a girl-band/dance troupe, so they were used to tight quarters."

"And why aren't you still hauling around pretty dancers, young man?" Bayjy asked in a schoolmarm kind of voice.

She didn't look much older than Valentinian, at least as far as Dave could tell, but she had the mannerisms down.

"It's complicated," Valentinian said. "Her old partner got involved, and things got a little out of hand. We bailed before the authorities decided to arrest everyone. At least the survivors."

"Kill 'em all and let God sort them out?" she asked knowingly.

"No," Dave leaned forward and smiled at her. "Only the ones that were in my way. I crippled the important one so he would remember me from the jail cell where he's going to spend the rest of his life."

She looked at him, and a little light came on in those black eyes.

"Shit," she ejaculated. "You're serious."

"There were only six of them," Dave smiled at her. "Five after the cop had stunned one. And they didn't see me coming in through the window."

"Well that would make me feel better," Bayjy breathed out. "There's some bad men and women out there."

She paused and looked at both of them in turn.

"So if I find you a cargo that pays decent, you'll hire me as a fixer?" she asked, point-blank and rather bluntly.

The outer door opened right then, with a team of wait staff delivering more bread, more drinks, and platters of ribeye cooked just to medium rare, so conversation halted.

"We'll talk," Valentinian told the woman amidst the hustle, but Dave knew the look in his eyes.

There was a treasure map he would want to research. And that would take a couple of days, and maybe buying and installing a new travel zone or two into the nav computer. And Vee had just won three thousand Union Krodageni playing poker, so he had money burning a hole in his pocket, or at least enough to goof off for a few days.

And a willing accomplice, if he wanted. If they wanted.

Valentinian would ask him, but Dave hadn't seen anything about the woman that would cause him to veto her. Plus he had developed those senses pretty well, in the Dominion Household where everyone wore masks both physical and metaphorical.

He had wanted an adventure. And he was pretty sure Vee did as well.

Bayjy was good enough people. At least for now.

Dave could always kill her himself if she decided to double-cross them later.

[5]
VALENTINIAN

VALENTINIAN WAS JUST glad he was by himself as he walked into the compact space and looked around. It wasn't a flashback to Dominion Prime, but maybe the exact opposite of déjà vu. Whatever that was.

He had never been here before, but he suddenly remembered sitting in that bar, just before Dave and Lianearia had blasted into his life, complaining to himself how all adventures seemed to start in bars and not libraries.

And yet, here he was, standing in the library, looking for adventure.

It had taken him a good part of a day to find this place, as the entire space station almost seemed to be built to obscure the fact that they even had a public library. He put that down to more things that the local middlemen could charge you for, as Laurentia was generally a friendly-enough place.

Just poor. Not all that many planets with tremendously valuable resources to export, except people. Plus, having the Dominion not all that far away had something to do with the fact that most planets maintained an active military reserve of every able-bodied person between sixteen and sixty training regularly. And a willingness to throw the entire planet at you if you tried to invade them.

Even the last couple of Dominators had finally taken a hint and gone after easier game than a pack of rabid chipmunks.

So places like this station traded what they could. And imported what they had to. A good chunk of cash came from training up people in excellent schools and sending them off to be doctors, nurses, or mercenaries somewhere else, with money sent home to support the extended families.

Not every place was poor, but Laurentian culture had a streak of vicious egalitarianism to it. You helped your neighbors, or they might decide you weren't part of society any more. And do bad things to you, perhaps with a mob of their poor friends.

Which brought him to a small, public library, hidden away. The locals, Valentinian was sure, all knew how to find it, but didn't want to tell the outsider, because then they could charge him for information that they could get for free.

Worse, there were a lot of books in here. He was positive that most of the information he needed would be electronic, but even then, there would probably be cultural references that would obscure things.

At least there was a woman seated behind a round counter, on a small dais, in the exact center of the space. Hopefully, the librarian. All of the computer screens faced in towards her so she could look over shoulders. She even looked like a librarian, straight out of central casting.

Somewhere in her mid-forties, was his first guess, with a decade possible either direction. Brown hair worn up in a bun. Reading half-glasses perched on her nose as she looked at some book he couldn't see from here. White shirt, buttoned up and starched to the point he thought he could smell it from here.

And maybe just the slightest hint of perfume underneath it. Maybe just left over from someone who had read a lot of books earlier.

She looked up with brown eyes that focused on him like a tracking sensor.

He expected a sniff of disapproval to find a stranger here, but she kept her feelings to herself for now.

They were alone in a space that would have held fifty comfortably.

"May I help you with something?" she asked in an arch, disbelieving voice.

Not entirely unfriendly, but not all that warm and welcoming, either.

But this was Laurentia. He did have one guaranteed way to get her attention.

"I hope so," Valentinian said earnestly as he approached. Might as well play dumb and polite. "I have a section of a larger star map without the normal triangulation coordinates, and was hoping that I might be able to use the computer systems here to find a close-enough match. That way I don't have to spend a lot of cash buying unnecessary additions to my ship's nav database."

As he got closer, Valentinian pulled out a forty

Union Krodageni note and rested it on the counter between them.

"If you have some time available, might I be able to pay you for some expertise and assistance?" he asked in a straightforward, businesslike tone.

This was Laurentia. Money was always short, except for the pampered few. He didn't figure a librarian would be in the latter category.

She fixed him with a hard stare, glancing at the cash long enough to note that it was almost as much as she was getting paid today, if he had done the conversions right.

"I'm from the Dominion, originally," he said with a polite smile. "Passing through. And I won a treasure map in a poker game."

If nothing else, he might entice her with that kind of a story. It was a pretty good one, for all that it sounded cliché.

"How good is your map?" she finally asked.

She still hadn't moved a hand to touch the money.

"Within parameters, pretty good," Valentinian said. "Seventy stars set in three dimensional relation to one at the center, with reasonable vectors."

"Then what seems to be the problem?" she asked, prim and superior finally starting to wake up and get a good look at him.

"That's a thirty-light-year sphere," Valentinian smiled back at her. "In a cube possibly five thousand light years across. With no idea how old the original of the map itself might be, so some of those stars may have drifted pretty hard since the map was laid down. Not much, but enough to not be a match, if I were to purchase that big of a nav database and then set my nav computer to crunching numbers for a month."

"What's at the center of the map?" she asked. He could see the first hints of intrigue in her eyes, a librarian with a mystery to solve and a lot of books handy.

"I have no idea," Valentinian let his weight shift to one side. "Like I said, I won it in a poker game yesterday. Farmer kid wasn't in a mood to talk, as the sheriff was in the process of arresting him and sending him somewhere else."

"That was you?" she asked, suddenly acting like a person and not a dismissive schoolmarm.

"If you mean, was I the guy that the sheriff used to clean the kid out in a semi-crooked poker game? Then yeah," he said. "Took all the kid's money, and he lost this map on top of it."

"So that's what he was trying to do," she said.

Valentinian looked at her curiously.

"Trouble maker," she said with an anger directed elsewhere, relaxing so much that he thought she might slump out of the chair. "Big and dangerous looking, but extremely young. Laurentian, so I had to offer to help, but he was so secretive and positively rude. Would always hide the screen and curse at me."

"Yup, that's him," Valentinian said. He pulled out the map and rested it next to the still-untouched money. "This."

She opened it and studied the map for several seconds.

"You won this in a poker game?" she asked, disbelieving.

Valentinian could see the woman reevaluating

him as she did. He wasn't sure if he was moving up or down the scale, but he just needed her brains, not her undying love or resolute friendship. Any addition to his nav computers was going to be expensive. Buying more than one was an ugly cost to consider. Best to do this right the first time.

So he told her about the game. Explained the sheriff's role. The stacked deck. That last hand. The raise over the top of the kid's pile that brought out what might have been his most valuable possession, and the one that brought him to town from the farm.

"And you gave him two hundred Union Krodageni?" she asked, shock evident in her tone.

"Well, one hundred to get him off the station, mostly to protect me from having to look over my shoulder," Valentinian corrected. "But yeah, the other hundred was because I've been there. He could at least eat for a month or six weeks if he was careful."

"For a total stranger?" she asked, eyes boring in.

"I had already made more money playing poker that night than I expected in a place like this, so it wasn't really my cash," he said truthfully. "I'm even happy to bribe you with his money, so we can solve the mystery of the map."

She paused and considered the bill sitting on the table.

"Okay," she decided. "Let's see what we can do here. Are you willing to let me scan it so I can run it through some systems?"

Valentinian considered that. It sounded like a perfectly reasonable request, but it also let the treasure out of his control, whatever it was. And he was feeling a little greedy, truth be told.

"How about you scan just this part?" he pointed. "Can I steal some tape and plas-paper?"

She handed him supplies, and Valentinian covered over the stack of numbers on the right side. Those were only useful once you found your target system, telling you where to actually go. Without them, nobody could get closer than the star system itself.

She scanned it and handed him back the map, which went into an inner pocket.

"Okay, let's see," she mused absently as she brought up the actual map and began letting some graphics program pull out the dots and vectors and translate them into relative grid coordinates.

She looked up, almost surprised to still find him standing there.

"I'm sorry," she said. "Got a little too into the process. I'm Stephaneria."

"Valentinian," he smiled. "Guesstimate on how long this will take?"

"A couple of hours for the automation to pull everything out and run a few smoothing routines to get close on the estimated locations," she sighed. "Then we can push it into a stellar repository system and ask for matches. I'm not sure how long that might take."

"Is there anything I can do, besides be in your way?" Valentinian asked.

"Probably not," she said. "It will be up to the computers to find anything, once I give it the parameters."

"Okay, then can I take you out to dinner as a way of saying thank you for your help?" Valentinian asked. "It's the kid's money, and I feel like spending it around here if I can."

"You're already paying me," her eyes got that look a woman's did when they thought you were on the verge of getting a little too personal.

"That was for your expertise," Valentinian let his own voice get a little sharp in response. "This is for your friendliness. I'm hoping to make this station something of a new base as my crew and I run cargo around. It would be pleasant to know some friendly people around here. You people can get a little insular around outsiders."

"Oh," she suddenly blushed. "I'm so sorry. I had thought-"

"I know what you thought, ma'am," Valentinian interrupted that thought. Not that it hadn't crossed his mind, but that wasn't why he was here. She was a nice-looking woman, even if she might be his mother's age. "I'd rather have friends around here."

"Yes. Sorry," she was utterly flustered now.

Did no man on this station have a librarian fetish? What was wrong with these people?

Before Valentinian could say anything, his card-reader beeped.

Dave.

Valentinian nodded to the woman and stepped back from the desk.

"What's up?" Valentinian asked as he opened it and keyed in the radio channel.

"I think it would be a very good idea if you returned to the ship right this moment," Dave said in a voice so utterly without emotion that Valentinian reached his other hand into his jacket to make sure the shock pistol was still there.

"Who just showed up?" Valentinian asked, making sure he had his map tucked away safely in a pocket and stepping backwards from the librarian as his flight or fight signals ramped up.

"Kyriaki Apokapes," Dave said, like a trumpet announcing the end of the world. "She is not alone."

Valentinian felt the bottom drop out of his soul, like a black hole pulling you down into eternity.

"I'll be along," Valentinian said. "Keep the ship locked up. Detach if you have to and come back for me later."

"Seriously, Vee?" Dave asked.

"They want you more than they do me, Dave," he replied, cutting the channel before the man could reply.

Stephaneria was looking at him with an odd mixture of humor and concern.

"Can I suddenly turn that dinner into a rain check?" he asked, backing another step away.

"Old girlfriend?" Stephaneria asked with a slight grin.

"It's complicated," Valentinian replied, hating himself for something so cliché being also so dead accurate. "She's also one of the Dominion's White Hats. The Internal Security Bureau. If someone comes here, my suggestion is you deny talking to me. Safer for you that way."

"That bad?" she asked, more concern coming to the fore. "You just told someone to take your ship and run."

"We're outside of Dominion space, so they have no legal jurisdiction," Valentinian said. He was clear to the door now. "And they know it. So anyone here has to be treated like a potential assassin instead."

"What did you do?" she asked before she caught herself. She had a really pretty blush that made him reconsider some things.

"The right thing," Valentinian finally answered over his shoulder as he opened the hatch and exited. "And they'll never forgive me for it."

[6]

VALENTINIAN

HE HAD MADE it about halfway to the ship when Valentinian's sneakier instincts woke up and poked his conscious brain. It was an idea so utterly daft and diabolical that he laughed out loud in a mostly-empty corridor.

Hopefully, nobody noticed.

Valentinian paused long enough to pull out his card-reader and call up a map of the station. Good, it wasn't that far out of his way. Hopefully, this would work.

Valentinian opened a channel to Dave as he started to jog down a side corridor.

"Where are you?" his first mate asked.

"In route," Valentinian answered. "You locked up tight and safe?"

"For the moment," Dave said. "Can you talk now?"

"In a corridor, heading to see if I can recruit some help," Valentinian replied. "Do you know where she is?"

"No," Dave admitted. "I paid a little extra to get the full data pull from the port authority on an automated basis, and then programmed some subroutines and set them to looking for certain names and locations, just so it would send us an alarm if it saw something."

"You can do that?" Valentinian was so shocked that he stopped moving.

One, that it could be done, although thinking about it, all that data was public somewhere. He had just never needed something like that before. Still wasn't used to thinking like a fugitive from justice. Or from an assassin, which was almost the same thing.

And Two, that Dave Hall was that facile with programming. The man had never suggested that sort of technical skill. Probably didn't want to give away too much about his former life, after Valentinian had purposefully not wanted to know. But he could probably use that.

"Yeah," Dave replied, with just a sniff of smugness that made it all the worse. The man could be a clown, when he wanted to be. "So I just got a flag that the Inspector was inbound, or had just docked. Not sure what the lag is between someone sending information in and it getting rebroadcast on the other circuit. How soon until you're here?"

"Need to make a stop," Valentinian said. "See a man about a horse. You keep everything locked down hard and I'll call before I try to open the hatch."

"Good enough," Dave said.

Valentinian tried not to giggle as he started to jog again. This one was about as insane as anything he had ever done in a half-decade of some amazingly bad decisions that should have turned out so much worse than they had.

Playing longshots.

There. Hopefully the man likes me, and doesn't just arrest me on general principles and hold me for her.

Valentinian opened the armored hatch and stepped into the station's primary security office. There was a deputy behind a heavy counter, the kind of structure that looked like it would stop any small arms a mob might be able to lay hands on.

Fortunately, Valentinian recognized the man from yesterday. One of the spacers in disguise that had arrested the punk.

The man acknowledged him as well.

"Something I can help you with?" he asked in the breezy tone of an authority figure dealing with a stranger in town.

"Is the sheriff available?" Valentinian asked politely. "Want to ask the man for a favor."

"Your name?" the deputy asked, nodding politely enough.

"Valentinian Tarasicodissa," he replied. "Tell him the poker player is here. The other poker player."

"Have a seat."

Valentinian moved over to a corner and sat on a bench probably designed to be uncomfortable enough to prevent sleep while you waited. He didn't fidget, or pull out his card-reader, but tried to work his way through any number of possible scenarios.

Not the least of which was how the hell that woman had managed to find them. He hadn't run as fast as he could, once they had cleared Dominion space, but they hadn't dawdled, either. She had to have set out on his trail almost immediately, and then slowly gained ground over the light centuries, only because he had slowed down, thinking he was safe.

Wouldn't ever make that mistake again.

He considered asking Stephaneria if they had any good political maps of what lay beyond Wildspace. The stars wouldn't change, but the people would. Hell, this far out from Cronus Prime, his own nav records were probably providing a pretty good update for other folks. Especially since the news of a murdered Dominator was only now starting to filter out.

Hopefully, nobody would make that obvious and potentially terminal connection.

"Captain," the deputy said. "He'll see you now. Leave your firearm with me."

Valentinian rose and pulled the shock pistol carefully enough as to not alarm the man. He swapped it for a receipt and got passed through a secured door into the inner portions of the sheriff's station.

It was nicer back here. Warmer, with wood paneling, house plants, and thick carpets, where the outer office had been metal walls and floors, like so much of the rest of the station.

This felt homey.

The old man was standing in a hatch on the far side of a bullpen filled with other deputies doing esoteric things. He nodded when Valentinian saw him and disappeared back into the office.

Valentinian followed.

Inside, it was more a man's study than a business office. Plants he couldn't recognize were potted in the near two corners. A sea of dark oak represented the biggest desk Valentinian could remember. Two black leather chairs bolted to the floor and a sofa in tan cloth along the right hand wall.

The man himself hadn't changed. Sixty or so. Lean as whipcord, and about as tough. Dressed in simple cotton rather than anything fancy, with a palm-sized badge over his heart.

"Thank you for your help yesterday, Captain," the sheriff began as Valentinian sat. "How can I help you?"

"So I'm not sure what story they're going to tell you when they arrive, but it'll be a doozy," Valentinian replied, sitting a little forward still. "And a complete fabrication, with just enough truth to it to sound believable enough."

"Who are they?" the man asked, never losing that friendly smile, even if it vanished out of his eyes.

"My first mate just pinged me that a ship was arriving or had arrived," Valentinian said. "I'm headed there now, but hoped I might ask you for a little bureaucratic interference. If it's really them, I plan to back away from the station as fast as I can get clearance, and vanish into the night as fast as my warpbubble will carry me."

"Will you now?" the man pressed, in a tone that suggested he could prevent that if he wanted. And they both knew it.

"Inspector Kyriaki Apokapes, Sheriff," Valentinian said. "That was the name that triggered my first mate. Dominion Security Bureau. The White Hats."

"Oh, my," the man had the most sarcastic way with words.

"She and I almost had a thing, back on Tartarus," Valentinian said. It was mostly true, since he hadn't stopped thinking about the woman in nearly four months, going back to Dominion Prime. But this was absolutely not the time to mention that bit. "If she's here, it's personal, rather than business. You strike me as one of the most honest cops I've ever known, in a short career of pushing my luck and trying to do the right thing. All I want to do is run some more. Don't want anybody hurt."

"I saw how you treated that kid, Captain," the old man nodded. "It was unnecessary for you to help him like that. That sort of things buys you some credibility here."

"I've been broke and far from home, Sheriff," Valentinian offered. "Wouldn't wish that on anyone, even an asshole like him. Just want to get gone now so my trouble doesn't have to spill out on your deck. People around here have been nice to me, so they don't deserve my grief. That make sense?"

"It does," the sheriff nodded. "Wondered how you'd react."

Oh?

Shit.

"Seems they knew you were here, and that young lady filed an official request to have you detained until she could take you and your first mate into custody," he said in an offhand manner.

And I'm very much disarmed in the presence of a man with one of the fastest gun hands I've ever seen.

Hopefully Dave runs.

"Oh," Valentinian said, leaning back and letting the chair finally take his weight.

It was very much out of his hands at this point.

"But, as you said, you've been trying to do the right thing since you got here," the man continued. "Even when it was unnecessary on your part. Looked at your behavior and you have been exceptional. And that's saying something here."

"So now what?" Valentinian said.

"So my niece called me after you left," the man's smile was grim, but friendly. "Asked if there was anything I could do to help."

"Your niece?" Valentinian completely lost the thread.

The only woman he'd been working with lately was Bayjy Endon, and the Sheriff was pure human, rather than one of the variants. Plus, Bayjy claimed to be a foreigner herself.

"Stephaneria," the man said. "The librarian."

Oh. Her. Huh.

"Her husband was a shit, so she divorced him and moved out here," the man said. "I got her a job as our librarian, because we needed one, and she needed a place to go. She called me after you left, and filled in the other half of the story, after I told her about the poker game last night over dinner."

"Ah," Valentinian said. "Well it looks like I won't be able to get her help with the map, since either we gotta run, or you're going to arrest us."

"Perhaps, young man," the sheriff said. "Just perhaps. The problem with kids is that they don't necessarily take the long approach to things."

"Sir?" Valentinian could feel that black hole tugging at his toes now.

"So perhaps you filed a flight plan to Meskle, Captain," the old man suggested. "Blast out of here without following proper procedures and all that, so we'd have to add a bunch of moving violations and fines, the next time you came through."

"Okay?" Valentinian tried to see where the man was going. "How does that help?"

"Well, I understand that your friend Endon was working on finding you a cargo," the Sheriff said. "And Stephaneria is involved now as well. If you looped out and circled back in about five or seven days, I'm pretty sure these Dominion folks might have also started chasing you by then. Then you might have enough time to pay off those traffic fines, load up a cargo, and maybe take my niece out to that dinner you promised, so you and your crew could then go looking for treasure."

"You sure, Sheriff?" Valentinian had to ask. "Might mean trouble for you and yours, long term."

"You were polite and friendly, Captain Tarasicodissa," the old man said.

"Valentinian," he corrected.

"Valentinian," the Sheriff smiled now, all the way to his eyes. He nodded in acknowledgement. "Them other folks come in loud and aggressive, threatening me and my station with all sorts of grief and trouble if we didn't jump to immediately. That sort of thing doesn't play well in Laurentia."

"Okay," Valentinian nodded. "What do I do?"

"You go board your ship, the *Longshot Hypothesis*," the Sheriff said. "File a flight plan and just leave, regardless of what the Stationmaster says. I'll square it with her later. And I'll talk to Endon and my niece, and we'll expect you back in a week. I'll leave a message at the outermost marker buoy if your friends haven't left yet, but if they've chased your asses this far, they won't tarry long here."

"Thank you, sir," Valentinian rose and shook his hand. "You know, for once trying to do the right thing might not be going to get me in trouble."

"You've been hanging out with the wrong sorts of folks, Valentinian," the old man also rose. His grip was firm. "Maybe you should spend more time here at Bohrne in the future?"

"I'll burn that bridge when we get there, Sheriff," Valentinian said. "Got a posse hot on my trail for a misunderstanding, and need to take care of that before anything else."

"Best of luck, young man," the Sheriff said with a warm smile.

Valentinian cleared the bullpen and picked up his shock pistol, almost running through the corridors.

"Update?" Dave asked as he answered the radio. "Don't see you on the camera, standing at the back door."

"Good news," Valentinian replied. "Will explain when I get there. You start a pre-flight right now. We've got some friends that are going to help."

"We've only been here three days, Vee," Dave sounded surprised. "How is that possible?"

Valentinian just laughed.

"Sometimes, the cards are stacked in your favor, big guy."

[7]
KYRIAKI

As starships went, Kyriaki found this one oddly comfortable, while at the same time still as militaristic as anything she had ever ridden on. But those others had been vessels of the Dominion Armada. Dedicated warships intended to frighten people who saw them on a scanner or out a porthole.

This one was something she might class as an assault courier, if pressed. Total operating crew around twenty, but she had only ever seen most of them as faces in a corridor, or doing things for Athanasia. Kyriaki was just a passenger, while the supposed *Widow* appeared to be in some sort of Supernumerary position, like a Tribune able to give orders to the captain.

Her meals had been either alone, or with the Widow and perhaps the captain, a faceless bureaucrat apparently chosen for his ability to disappear from your mind the moment he left your sight. Probably useful on a small ship like this.

They had left Dominion space behind. Kyriaki had almost felt that transition in her bones, deep in the warpbubble carrying them. One moment, law and order. The next, what?

Depending on how you interpreted things, they might now be verging on being interstellar pirates. Criminals of some sort, since the intent was to kill or at least capture the man known publicly as Dave Hall and haul at least his body home for public ridicule, prior to execution.

While possibly never admitting who the man really was.

The Widow also seemed to be intent on killing anyone who knew the truth, and that was where the trouble would start. Athanasia would have to capture Valentinian and put the truth serum to the man, to see what he knew. Which would eventually lead the Widow to a cop having a crisis of conscience. One that hadn't gotten any better after she learned more of the truth that she had only suspected before.

Worse, perhaps, since Kyriaki could have taken Dave in when he offered. She would have been promoted and celebrated had she done so.

And miserable. She knew that much. He really had just wanted out. After two weeks in the close company of the Widow, Kyriaki was beginning to understand why, although the older woman might be more of a shrew in her grief and anger than she had been before.

Kyriaki doubted it, since something had driven the man to becoming Dave Hall. It might be sitting across the conference table right now.

"You have the most field experience, Inspector,"

the Widow said. "How would you approach this situation?"

It was just the two of them right now in this conference room, although there was a team of six agents aft that had kept largely to themselves. They weren't Kyriaki's people, so she wasn't sure how they would move. She was pretty sure none of them would have the slightest compunction about shooting her if the Widow suddenly ordered it.

Which she might.

"We have chased them hard and far, ma'am," Kyriaki said. She had stopped calling the woman by her given name at some point, and didn't have a proper title to fall back on. Calling her *Widow* to her face was just rude. "If they have enough paranoia, and they might, they'll run as soon as we catch up with them again, even though *Longshot Hypothesis* has left a clear trail to date."

"Will they go beyond Laurentia?" the Widow asked.

Kyriaki had to shrug. She really didn't know Valentinian all that well as a person, so much as a semi-fantasy that haunted her dozing hours like a dangerous ghost. And just the desire to run her fingers through the man's hair angered her almost as much as it excited her.

But she reminded herself that protecting the man at this point was just a case of protecting herself as well. Nothing more than that. Regardless of what her body might suggest.

At least the Ambassador wasn't here, to witness what might have to come next. The betrayal of everything the White Hats stood for. They weren't assassins. They were cops.

But killing both Dave Hall and Valentinian Tarasicodissa before they could talk to anyone from the Dominion would solve most of Kyriaki's problems. Might create others, but she would just have to deal with those as they arrived.

"This vessel is armed, correct?" Kyriaki took the conversation a different direction.

"Not as well as a larger warship," Athanasia replied. "But it is my understanding that *Longshot Hypothesis* is not?"

"That is the case," Kyriaki said. "At least at present. While the captain might have wanted to change that, they had not stopped anywhere long enough to have that level of work done. So you can credibly threaten them, either firing a shot across their bow, or attempting to disable the ship by shooting out one or both engines, if it becomes necessary."

"We can, yes," the Widow nodded. "I would rather see this Dave Hall person in the flesh, though, so I can confirm it is him and not yet another cypher, while my husband has disappeared again."

That stopped her cold. Kyriaki had been working on the assumption that Dave had remained with Valentinian. Would remain with him. Could the man have hired someone else in Dave's place and doctored the records? This was Laurentia, not the Dominion. Records were less sacrosanct here.

"I have an idea, then," Kyriaki rolled the dice in her head and bet heavily. Not everything, but enough. This situation would only get worse, if this woman was that intent on seeing it through to the bitterest dregs.

She waited for the Widow to nod before

proceeding. Kyriaki was still just an Inspector on detached duty. Serving now at the whim of the Dominion Household itself, and a woman about to lose a significant chunk of the prestige she had known for the last twenty-five years.

There is nothing as dangerous as a woman scorned. Even Kyriaki was just protecting her career and her life. Athanasia would possibly be settling old scores, because nothing would ever make her the wife of a Dominator again. Only the *Widow*.

Athanasia had the look of a woman supremely intent on making that man pay the ultimate price.

"Go ahead," the Widow said brittlely when Kyriaki didn't immediately respond.

"If we do find them at Bohrne, we should immediately contact the authorities, as soon as we come out of warp, and file fugitive paperwork so they will hold them, or at least the ship," Kyriaki offered.

"And if they run at that moment?" the Widow asked. "Just because the stationmaster orders them to remain is no guarantee. They might just flee immediately."

"Yes," Kyriaki agreed. "And as soon as we dock, I will slip out the side airlock, traverse the exterior of the station, and sneak aboard *Longshot Hypothesis*. The vessel's secondary personnel airlock is located forward, just off the bridge, so I should be able to disable the vessel, or at least surprise them in the act of fleeing and force them to heave to."

"That will be dangerous," the Widow said. "Should you go alone, or take the team?"

"One person may not be noticed by station personnel," Kyriaki replied. "Half a dozen will. And none of them have been aboard *Longshot Hypothesis*. It is not a Dominion vessel, but an Anuradhan cargo transport. Much of the architecture is oddly arranged and designed. Plus, I will take a detonator with me, on a deadman switch. If they choose to commit suicide, then at least the scales will be balanced."

"You do not generally strike me as the Death Or Glory type, Inspector," the Widow questioned her more closely. "Why are you doing this?"

"That man has dishonored the entire Dominion, Athanasia," Kyriaki ground out the words. This, at least, was the honest truth. "Everything I stood for. Stand for. Were you planning to take him home and call off the Tournament of Domination?"

That was a low blow, and Kyriaki knew it, but she needed the woman's anger at the fore now, and not decades of personal calculations and maneuvering.

"No," the older woman said. "Dave Hall must die. Captain Tarasicodissa as well. I would like to ask the man why he did this, but I can also settle for not knowing for the rest of my life if you have to kill him when we arrive. Are you prepared to die?"

"I do not plan to let them win," Kyriaki said simply, leaving the *they* part ambiguous. "What happens if we fail here and they flee into Wildspace?"

"That man cannot ever flee far enough that I will stop chasing him," the Widow's anger was hot now. "Nor convince me to spare him. As you said, an insult to the entire Dominion, but also to me, personally. I have been dishonored so badly that no amount of blood will ever wash it clean."

Kyriaki nodded. Now the stakes were on the table.

She could always kill Dave Hall and return home a hero. All she had to do was kill Valentinian, too.

———

"INSPECTOR, we are about to come out of warp in the Bohrne system," the voice came out over the comm system.

Kyriaki had been reading a recent history of Laurentia that she had downloaded at the last station where they had chased *Longshot Hypothesis*. The population here was almost as militant as the Dominion, but most of that was a cultural response to a near neighbor like the Dominator.

Had they really mobilized an entire population as guerillas to overcome a planetary invasion? The Dominion wanted to conquer worlds, when they couldn't absorb them peacefully. You could hold orbit with a fleet, but what good did that do you if you had to end up bombarding the cities below you? And while the Caelons, the Dominion's Assault Cavalry, were the finest troops in the known galaxy, would the Laurentians really accept one thousand casualties to kill just each one?

But then, perhaps you needed *Le Beau Geste*, the Grand Gesture, to convince the Dominator to leave you alone. Dave Hall had, after a few raids early in his reign.

A man who understood impossible situations.

"Heading aft now," Kyriaki opened the channel and responded.

She made her way to the airlock bay and located the suit she would wear. Unlike Anuradhan vessels, with the engines forward on wings, Dominion vessels kept theirs centerline rear. The airlock bay was not far in front of that.

It would give *Longshot Hypothesis* a head start, if he ran. Valentinian could just unlock from the station and push his engines, while the assault courier had to back away on local thrusters vectoring from the rear engines, rotate once they were clear, and only then give chase.

Kyriaki hadn't seen the full specs on Valentinian's chariot, but she suspected that he could outrun them both in real space as well as in a warpbubble. The original flight path from Dominion Prime to Aestrolathia had been something that only a courier like this one could have matched for elapsed time.

But she didn't tell the Widow that. Too much of a risk that the woman would just park in front of *Longshot Hypothesis* and blast it with a particle cannon while the ship was still docked.

Kyriaki needed to solve this issue at a very personal level. With a shiv, as it were, rather than a sledgehammer.

While Kyriaki got into the suit and attached all the various plumbing necessary for a long visit, she felt the ship drop out of the warpbubble and rotate to decelerate into the station at Bohrne.

Again, *Longshot Hypothesis* would have a small advantage. Right now, they were facing out, and could chase, but at some point, the courier would have to turn nose-in to align the primary personnel airlock with the station. This courier didn't have a cargo deck, so there was no big door involved.

She was suited and waiting. Seated on a bench with her faceplate open and air and power lines coming out of a wall to keep her topped up.

Contemplating the two detonators tucked carefully into external belt pouches. Occasionally touching the heavy stun pistol on her thigh outside the semi-armor of her suit.

The suit itself wasn't all that bulky, but it was still an alien experience. She was fully certified in it, but had rarely had to do something like this to catch a criminal or plotter. Mostly, they were surprised in bed and taken into custody while in their pajamas.

The Widow entered the chamber and approached. She was dressed in her finest robes today, like this was a funeral. Which it was, in ways that had not been sorted out.

Or rather, *whose funeral* was still on the table.

"Inspector," she acknowledged as she got close. "You are sure?"

"There is no other way," Kyriaki said. "Perhaps we will be lucky and they will be off ship and the local authorities can arrest them with minimal effort, but I have my doubts."

"And you will storm this ship by yourself?" Athanasia asked.

"All I have to do is toss one of these into the bridge," Kyriaki replied, touching the pocket with the detonator. "The controls will be disabled enough that they cannot flee, because there are no other flight controls on the vessel. If the two men are in there, they'll die with the ship. If not, they'll be taken."

"Very good, then," the Widow said. "I wish you luck in your mission. I would like to see Dave Hall once more, but I will settle for his corpse."

She nodded and departed, leaving Kyriaki alone with her thoughts.

"Inspector, on final approach now," a voice came over her radio.

Kyriaki acknowledged and closed up, unplugging everything and moving into the airlock itself. The inner door closed with a thump and the room hissed like a deflating ball as it fell to vacuum.

She checked her systems, but everything was green.

Deep breath.

Kyriaki triggered the outer hatch and waited as it irised open into six sections on massive pistons. She grabbed a stanchion and leaned out far enough to study the station. From here, it looked like a wall that disappeared in all directions. Another vessel was docked in the next space over, but most of this deck was for cargo, and most cargo ships didn't bother with portholes.

The courier, *Dominion-427*, docked with a kiss. The hull shuddered as clamps locked on and an airlock extended to embrace the bow of the courier.

Kyriaki waited until the docking was complete, and then slipped out of her space. She quickly got to the outer skin of the station on backpack thrusters, and then clamped her magnetic boots to the hull.

It might be faster to fly there directly, but someone would notice her. Even short-range collision sensors would trigger if she was moving around, and then she would have to deal with the stationmaster and whoever else.

But a bug walking on the surface of the station would hopefully be ignored.

Her system chirped once and a map appeared on a right-hand side screen. The courier was in green. *Longshot Hypothesis* was in red. Not all that far away, but she would have gladly circumnavigated the entire exterior of the station to get to those men.

There was much that needed to be discussed.

All they had to do was wait for her to arrive.

And then, she could confront her problem.

[8]

DAVE

DAVE KEPT a set of camera views handy on the console in front of him, to try to stay on top of the developing situation. He had lots of experience with juggling a dozen catastrophes in his head at once.

Invading a planet gave one extremely good experience at that.

So he had cameras in both the cargo bay and the rear airlock, just in case somebody somehow managed to overcome the security systems aft and open either door, and to somehow manage that without setting off alarms. In addition, he had a feed from the station itself showing the deck just outside of the ship, to see who might be about to ring the doorbell with a gun in their hand.

Valentinian would be back soon. Or he would call. Or the White Hats would show up and Dave would just have to blast free and run like hell.

Would he come back later? Vee had specifically said they might arrest him and that Dave should escape.

There was always the option of another rescue, but he had needed the woman's help the first time. If the White Hats had come this far, they knew the truth, and he could expect that the woman was going to kill him this time.

Except she already knew the truth. Had guessed part of it on Tartarus, and he had volunteered the rest. So it made no sense that she was here now, unless more of her people had arrived on Tartarus just after he and Valentinian had left, and she had gotten swept up in their wake.

Or she had changed her mind about arresting him. Never leave that option off the table when talking about a woman. She might have woken up the next morning and decided the galaxy would be a better place without he and Valentinian in it.

Just in case, Dave had checked out a flame pistol from the armory, as well as a pulse carbine. If the White Hats managed a breach, they would be gunning for bear, and Dave knew there was no way in hell he wanted to be taken alive.

Not by those people. Even random pirates would only kill him.

The Dominion, if they were truly here, would want so much more than that.

So he was about halfway through the pre-flight checklist. Maybe running it a little faster than he needed to, but this was not a lazy Sunday afternoon. Bad people with guns would be here soon enough.

At the same time, Valentinian never cut corners on maintenance and work. And wouldn't allow Dave to do so, either. In a crunch, he could just unlock from the station, bring the engines up to one percent power and accelerate away, gradually pouring on the speed until he was clear enough to bubble into warp and disappear forever.

If he was lucky.

There were other identities he could use, in a pinch. Not as well documented as Dave Hall, and he would have to give up a significant portion of the money he had stashed away under Dave's picture, but it would be possible to do.

He would probably have to sell *Longshot Hypothesis* as part of his escape anyway. Even without Valentinian, the ship was still too well known in certain places, but it would give him the cash he needed.

But it would also mean abandoning his only friend in the galaxy to suffer what should have been *his* fate. That sort of thing absolutely galled him more than everything else.

What kind of man was he, if Valentinian had to be sacrificed? Not one he'd want to know.

"Longshot Hypothesis, this is Station Control," a woman's voice suddenly came over the line he had been monitoring. "Your flight plan for Meskle is received and acknowledged. Transmitting your outbound lane assignment now."

There was a file attached. Dave opened it and sure enough, lane assignment. Almost a straight shot outward from their current bow. Minimum time flight to the buoy.

How was that possible? Dave hadn't filed anything.

Unless Vee had.

Valentinian had mentioned friends that would help. Had he managed to bribe the stationmaster? Could they really pull this off?

"Uhm. Uh. Roger that, Station Control," Dave finally managed, still a little bewildered.

But Valentinian had charisma. That was one of the big reasons Dave had picked the young man. He had a record of getting into trouble, and somehow almost always being able to talk his way out of it.

Take that poker game, for instance.

Okay, then. Nothing to do now but finish the checklist and hope that Vee got here before that woman did. He put his nose down and toggled the secondary, port-side, thruster control on. Almost done.

His card-reader beeped, rather than the comm.

Vee.

"Yeah?" Dave asked.

"Standing close on the dock, but out of sight," Valentinian said quietly. "Don't see anything. But I don't trust anybody right now. Can you come aft and meet me in the personnel airlock with a pistol, just in case?"

"Be right down," Dave said.

He rose and checked the cockpit one last time. All the big parts of the pre-flight were done, with just minor bits remaining, if they were really in a hurry.

Out the door, across the rec room, and up the steps, through the engineering spaces to the cargo deck.

It was always weird to his sensibilities that the big space was off-center from the line of the ship. The ship was about thirty-two meters wide down the leg of the Y. But the rear airlock was four meters wide down the starboard side and the bay itself about twenty-eight, with two sets of tracks in the deck to load a pair of the big cargo boxes, ten meters by ten by thirty, with two meters of space between them.

He went into the rear airlock, but left the inner hatch open, so he could hear anything happening in the main bay. A quick, fisheye lens check at a local screen showed nobody standing outside the door, so Dave triggered the hatch, standing off to one side, more or less hidden by a spare hard suit hanging from a rack.

The door beeped loudly, to warn anyone to get out of the way, so there was no way to do this quietly. That was why there was a pulse carbine with the safety off in his hands. Someone rushing this door would be blown backwards if he shot them from this range, and possibly on fire.

Which would teach anyone who survived to be more polite in the future. Or try this stunt while wearing Caelon armor.

There was always that.

A shadow appeared at the door and Dave centered the carbine on them.

"Dave?"

Valentinian.

"Here," he murmured, just loud enough for the man to turn and see him.

"Good."

Vee stepped on the deck and slammed his palm onto the close button. He also drew a shock pistol and turned to watch the gap as the door began closing with more beeps.

Dave stayed perfectly still and watched.

Finally, the hatch sealed.

Valentinian let go a huge sigh and turned to the

locking mechanism. Dave couldn't see what he was doing, but it was probably good.

"Okay, nobody's opening this door," he said. "Just shut down power to both external pads. They'll have to cut it open if they want in."

He turned and Dave could see the stress of the last hour on the young man's face. Lines of exhaustion that hadn't been there at breakfast.

"We ready to go?" Vee asked.

Dave stepped away from the wall, set his safety on the weapon, and nodded.

"Almost through the checklist, but we could move if we had to," Dave said, turning and starting to jog. Vee would want to be on the bridge. "And Station Control already acknowledged our departure and sent us a lane assignment. What's up with that?"

"Told you," Valentinian was jogging with him. "We've got friends here. And if all goes well, we'll come back and see them in about a week, assuming the Dominion keeps chasing us when we leave here."

THE BRIDGE of *Longshot Hypothesis* was really the only place in the universe that Valentinian felt like calling home. Sure, he could go visit his parents, if he wanted a lecture from Dad about ruining his life, or for Mom to discuss all the eligible daughters of friends she knew.

Deep space was so much more welcoming than men and women who have already surrendered to old age and entropy.

Dave had gotten everything close to ready. Valentinian took a quick moment to verify a few things that always stuck or fussed on launch, but he could do this right now if he wanted to. Had to.

Valentinian decided to help Dave finish the checklist as a way of saying thank you for being competent. This would have been so much more of a pain in the ass from a dead cold start.

"Station this is *Longshot Hypothesis*," Valentinian said into the comm.

It helped that he was hard linked to the station and didn't have to announce to the universe what he was about to do. "Departure imminent."

Rather than wait for them to acknowledge, Valentinian cleared the locks aft with a sound like a vault door setting posts and puffed away from the station as soon as the bolts had retracted. The Dominion ship had docked, which he thought was a mistake. They should have parked right off his bow, because he was pretty sure they had guns and he didn't.

Of course, Laurentia might see that as an act of official piracy, since the vessel flew a Dominion Diplomatic flag.

The station would probably shoot back.

Not that it would un-destroy *Longshot Hypothesis* if those people were as serious at being crazed, militant, warrior monks like the guy sitting next to him, but maybe they didn't want to die today.

"Strap yourself in," Valentinian ordered his first mate. "This might get stupid."

Dave just nodded and began pulling his harness into place. Valentinian did the same, pausing to stab at buttons as he got enough clearance to not scorch metal behind him.

The engines were already warm and live. Now they began to push.

Most transports were designed to run cheap, so the engines had just enough power to move the vessel around and a warpbubble good enough to get you between stars in a reasonable amount of time.

Valentinian had always suspected that the previous owner had not just been a gearhead, but also a smuggler of some sort. The man had tuned the two engines significantly better than the factory had, a century and a half ago. And upgraded them to bigger models than the ship had originally shipped with.

These were off a vessel at least a third again heavier than the *Longshot*. The warpbubble generator was also an after-factory upgrade.

Valentinian didn't complain, but he occasionally wondered just what the hell that other guy had bought when he sold this beast.

But right now, it was time to go zoom. Valentinian pushed the engines a little harder. The Sheriff might claim that the fines would be reviewed later, but Valentinian really didn't care. He was only fifty/fifty on coming back here, anyway, in spite of what he had told the man, or his niece. Or Bayjy.

He might miss the purple lady the most, only because she was probably the most useful, going forward into the darkness of Wildspace.

"*Longshot Hypothesis*, this is *Dominion-427*," an angry voice came over the external radio. "You are ordered to heave to and prepare to be boarded, under Dominion Law."

Valentinian couldn't resist. He jumped the thrusters up another five percent and keyed the radio.

"This isn't the Dominion, buddy," he challenged. "That might be interpretable as a deliberate act of piracy in the sovereign space of Laurentia. They'll probably take offense."

Then he opened the engines up a little more. Taunting might actually cause them to do something stupid. But he just couldn't help himself.

From the grin on Dave's face, the big guy didn't mind all that much, either.

Behind them, the station receded at an ever-increasing clip. The fines would probably be ugly, but he could always plead mitigating circumstances. He hadn't done anything else illegal in Laurentian space. And the folks on *Dominion-427* would have to make some seriously crazy, PUBLIC, claims about Dave Hall being a wanted assassin if they wanted any sympathy.

Of course, the man who had just assassinated their worst enemy in the universe might be a hero here. Kinda the reason Valentinian had fled into Laurentia in the first place, rather than someplace like Asherah or Lei-Zu where the local cops might actually listen.

Boom. Zip. Away.

It was almost like living in a comic book.

Right up until the point that the access alarms went off on the forward airlock. The one right beyond the bulkhead next to Dave.

What the hell was going on? And of course he hadn't disabled that one when he did the two in back. Nobody had tried to break in that way in more than a year.

Plus, they were in deep space, heading away from Bohrne's station as fast as *Longshot Hypothesis* felt like running.

Valentinian keyed the camera live in the airlock as the door continued to open. He silenced the alarms, and put a hand on Dave's arm before the big guy could finish unbuckling his harness.

"Hang tight," Valentinian said, keying a couple of commands he hadn't told Dave about earlier.

In the wall, a little switch opened and cut power to the inner airlock hatch. Someone could still open it manually, by twisting the wheel that would push the inner hatch in, but they weren't getting in quickly that way. And he and the killer next to him were armed.

"What just happened?" Dave asked.

"I added a breaker override to the power lines on all the airlocks after the last time someone tried this exact trick," Valentinian said. "Except I was docked to a station at the time. He thought he'd be cute, but didn't quite understand how Anuradhan tech works, so managed to lock himself out of the bridge when he thought he was unlocking the hatch instead. There's a reason you see me with a shock pistol, even aboard the ship."

"Firefight inside *Longshot Hypothesis*?" Dave asked.

Most of the time, Valentinian didn't really like that look of glee that came into Dave's eyes when they talked about gunfire. Now, however…

"Yup," Valentinian answered him. "So there's a second set of alarms on all the airlocks. And some overrides."

"Can they still manage to get in?" Dave asked, almost hopeful from that gleam.

"Only manually, with the wheel, Dave," Valentinian nodded.

"Fish in a bucket," Dave smiled.

Valentinian shrugged and toggled some external cameras to try to see what was going on. The cockpit stuck out from the Y at the center of the ship, and that airlock was back a little ways, so he supposed that maybe one of them could push his nose up against the windshield and maybe see what was back there, but whoever it was had been trying to hide or they might already have been seen.

Probably thought they were still invisible, since the primary alarm hadn't gone off.

He looked and sure enough there was an override in place on the system alarms. One he didn't recognize, but *Longshot Hypothesis* did.

Like maybe the White Hats had insisted that all Dominion ships have a secret back door buried in their code base? Interesting.

Maybe he'd see if Dave was good enough to locate it, once they got rid of the pest.

Finally, Valentinian found a view that showed a single figure, suited up and lurking under the starboard wing, near where the landing gear pistoned down. Good spot to hide.

He would need to add a few more external cameras at the next planetary landing.

But there was only one figure.

And the door was fully open now, so the figure slid along the skin of the ship and got himself into the airlock professionally enough. Couple of buttons and the hatch began to seal itself up.

"How close are we to a warpbubble?" Dave asked.

He tapped the screen between them to show that *Dominion-427* had backed away from the station and was in the process of turning around to give chase.

"Close enough," Valentinian decided. They were just getting away from the station, so he didn't need that accurate of a plot for the Overdrive systems. Just enough to miss big things at FTL speeds for the next few hours.

He punched the button and the stars suddenly streamed into lines as the warpbubble took hold and cast them across the galaxy.

Longshot Hypothesis, running for the border.

In his forward airlock, their new passenger had gotten the outer hatch locked shut and an atmosphere inflated. Valentinian switched his view to the interior and watched the figure reach up and open their faceplate enough to test the air.

Valentinian was in a bad mood.

"You're trespassing," he announced into the airlock, after dialing the volume on the speakers up a few notches, just in case the intruder wasn't paying attention.

The intruder turned to face the inner hatch with his faceplate closed again and studied the barrier. He had a holster on his right thigh, with a weapon in it, but made no move to draw it.

Moments passed while the figure stood perfectly still. Valentinian couldn't detect any radio transmissions, but they were inside a warpbubble right now, so his friends couldn't help him anyway.

He surprised Valentinian by reaching up and undocking his helmet, rotating it enough to detach, then hanging it from the lanyard that kept suit and helmet together at times like this.

Oh, shit.

Inspector Apokapes.

"Is that…?" Dave asked, almost as shocked.

"Yup," Valentinian replied.

He dialed the volume back down to normal conversation and keyed the button.

"What are you doing here, Inspector?" he asked.

She grimaced. The camera was good enough to watch, in spite of a slight fisheye.

"Saving your life, Dave's life, and mine," she replied in a flat, almost angry tone. "Permission to come aboard?"

WITH A SPACESUIT fully inflated inside a regular atmosphere, the skin will frequently act like a drum. Kyriaki discovered that the hard way.

Her head was ringing with Valentinian's words. At least he had turned it down the second time, or she might be facing an audio migraine later.

"Are you insane?" Valentinian asked, shock at war with anger in his voice.

"I can explain, but you need to get into warp right now," she replied. "Otherwise, we're all dead."

"Three steps ahead of you, lady," the captain snarled.

Good. His paranoia hadn't deserted him. Maybe they could all survive this, at least long enough to sort it all out.

"Is Dave still with you?" she asked, finding the camera on the inner wall he was probably watching through.

There was a long pause. She attributed it to the

comm being off and a conversation on the other side of the wall on her right.

"He is," Valentinian was back. "What's going on?"

"Dave, have you told him the truth yet?" Kyriaki asked in a hard voice.

Every second she was out here they were all at risk, but Valentinian could just kill her easy enough. Blow open the airlock in warpspace and it might suck her out and deposit her in the permanent darkness between stars, never to be found. She would become a frozen asteroid for some future archaeologist to discover. And none of this would be her problem anymore.

More silence. Longer this time. She could imagine the two men getting a little testy, but they might as well have it all out now, if they hadn't before.

Too much was at risk if Valentinian still thought Dave was just a fugitive. Or an assassin.

"Hello, Kyriaki," Dave's voice came on the line. "Why is that important right now? What's going on that puts you here and us there?"

"I rode out here on a Dominion Diplomatic Courier, Dave," she said matter-of-factly. Dave didn't need to know her opinion of several weeks with Athanasia. He probably shared them.

"And?" Dave asked.

"And the woman giving orders on that vessel went by the name of Athanasia, Dave," she replied.

Again silence. Probably Dave explaining what that name meant to Valentinian.

Kyriaki considered putting her helmet back on, but what good would that do her? Dying in hours instead of minutes? She could always just pull one of those detonators out of a pouch and end it all right now. The airlock was probably going to be reinforced to the point that it would hold.

All she would accomplish was splattering her own blood all over the walls and making one of those men have to come clean it up.

She was going to have to live or die on their decision.

"Describe her," Dave ordered in an angry, taut voice.

"Valentinian's height, give or take," Kyriaki replied. "Blond braid down to her kidneys. Broad shoulders and hips. Narrow waist. Shrill harpy of a woman. Said she knew you from the old days. Knew you rather well."

"She did," Dave said. "Stand by."

More silence.

This airlock had the look of little use. Probably only ever got opened when the ship was on the ground and Valentinian didn't feel like going out the main airlock aft.

Four suits of various sizes hung from racks and were locked in tight to their plugs. Three of them were simply skin suits, while the last one had the semi-plate, armored look of a cargo lifter. Valentinian's size, so they hadn't found one to fit Dave. Those would be hard to find. Probably have to custom order it.

The walls in her new prison were a cold, stark white, with lightbars on all eight sides of the octagonal tube. Why this one was octagonal instead of square made no sense to her, but this ship wasn't Dominion tech. They might have had a logical design, those people. Or a cultural one.

Kyriaki wondered about the conversation those two men were having right now. She apparently still knew more than Valentinian did about who Dave Hall really was.

All she had to do was kill both men, so that the truth could never get out.

Easy, right?

That was why she had spent so much time on the flight out here trying to find an outcome that didn't end up with either of them taken prisoner and subject to truth serum.

She'd be dead if they were. Plus, thoughts of Valentinian Tarasicodissa still haunted her in ways that set her body at war with itself. Killing him, as much as she might occasionally want to wipe that damned, smug smile off his face, wouldn't fix that.

So she had to destroy her old life. And hope she could figure out how to create a new one. Something that no longer involved the burgundy and white that had defined her for the last decade.

Out of the frying pan…

"Inspector?" Dave's voice intruded on her before she managed to squirrel in on that line of thought and get lost inside.

"Yes?" she asked as his voice trailed off.

"While we'd like to believe you, Valentinian still has some hard-held concerns, and I sort of agree with him," Dave said.

"Okay?" Kyriaki said, expecting the outer door to open to space on her.

At least it would be swift.

"In order to let you aboard the ship, we're going to need you to strip completely, and then we're going to jettison your suit," Dave said. "That way we're comfortable you don't have any weapons, and there is no tracking signal, even one you're not aware of."

She hadn't considered that Athanasia might have put a beacon on her suit. In addition to the regular emergency transmitter she could have used had she blown up the bridge and perhaps killed the two men. Or at least Valentinian's horse.

It made perfect sense. Without a beam weapon and surprise, she was probably no threat at all to Dave, and not much of one to someone as keyed up as Valentinian was going to be, at least until she convinced him she meant no harm.

What did she mean?

She still didn't know that either, and that left her raw and a little angry.

Kyriaki shrugged at herself and began to unhook latches and seams. It would be a pain in the ass, doing this by herself, but they weren't going to let her aboard the ship if she had a bomb hidden, which she did.

This took away all temptation to just kill them both and try to get her life back on track. Not that she ever would have. Letting Dave go on Tartarus had been the right thing to do. Nothing would change that. Even her second thoughts.

And she wasn't going to lie to herself about her attraction to Valentinian. Not that she might ever tell the man, if he didn't figure it out on his own.

Worst case, she could always walk away at their next landfall and steal someone's identity herself, like Dave had done.

By the time she got out of the suit and all the plumbing bits detached, Kyriaki was shivering with cold. She told herself that was it.

Not emotions, no.

Not barely-controlled rage. Not embarrassment at meeting these two men completely nude, to be inspected like a side of meat and maybe disposed of just about as emotionally. Not fear at what the hell she had done, leaving both detonators in the suit, along with the pistol, and surrendering herself to two of the most wanted fugitives in the galaxy.

Not walking away from Kyriaki Apokapes, and never being able to look back.

Never going home again.

In the end, she supposed that put them on a level playing field. Dave Hall wasn't even really Dave Hall. And Valentinian was going to go down in history as his accomplice, regardless of the actual truth.

The inner hatch began to beep. She stood before it proud, head up, shoulders back, daring the two men to say or do anything when they saw her, even if they had been watching the entire bizarre burlesque on a screen from the bridge.

Valentinian was standing close when the hatch cleared. Dave was clear across the room, watching, but not close enough she could do anything to him if she suddenly went berserk in the confines of the ship's rec room.

She stepped across the line in the deck and came to rest in front of the captain, naked, cold, and angry.

"You're insane. You know that, right?" Valentinian asked her with a curious, almost-grin.

He thrust a bundle into her hands and stepped back. It took her a moment to process. One of his T-shirts, plus a warm Henley and heavy ship's pants. Clothing for her to wear.

The table was up, so she put everything on the surface and pulled the shirt on.

"So I have considered," she finally replied as she pulled her head clear and reached for the pants. "This is not the logical response to the entire situation."

"So why?" Valentinian asked. "Why did you let Dave go, knowing the truth on Tartarus? Why volunteer to board *Longshot Hypothesis* and most likely get killed? Or kill us? What is going on?"

The pants were just the right fit, but that was because he was taller than her, while she was all leg. In fact, everything fit, once she rolled up the sleeves of the Henley two turns.

Dave stepped away from the wall now, handing her a closed mug of something that smelled like coffee. Whatever, it was warm. She needed warmth right now, so she popped one of the seats up and took it, finally relaxing for the first time in nearly a day.

The coffee had been spiked with a little something. Rum, maybe. It settled into her stomach and started to break up the cold spot that had taken root.

"Because I knew the truth." She finally looked up at Valentinian and nodded to Dave. "Not even you knew. But if they ever caught one of you, the truth serum would sign my death warrant, as well as yours. Every day was one more opportunity for someone to ask why I hadn't arrested the two of you on Tartarus, since my mission had been to investigate your background and find out why I didn't believe all the cover stories Dave had assembled."

She turned to the quiet man, watched him smile

down at her and take a seat across the table. Both he and Valentinian were still armed, but she didn't care.

This might be what rebirth felt like.

"You assembled the most amazingly complicated shell game I have ever seen, Dave," she told the man. "They would have been years before they finally unraveled it. My own superiors and Athanasia both told me that. I went and ruined it."

"How?" Valentinian asked. "Why?"

"I wanted to get inside your head and wipe that smug grin off your face," Kyriaki said to him quietly. "It had nothing to do with Dave, but the more I thought about you, the more the rest of the whole situation rang enough of a false note that I couldn't let it go. After I learned the truth, I made sure the two of you got off-planet as soon as possible, and disappeared. I had planned to write the whole thing down as the ongoing feud between Cleray and Nash in my final report, but the Ambassador of Dominion Prime and Athanasia showed up the next day, maybe five hours after you lifted. From there, I had no maneuvering room."

"So now what?" Valentinian asked carefully. "Dave explained to me who he used to be. And you apparently knew. And his wife, ex-wife, widow, something, is now chasing us across the galaxy."

She was glad that both men missed some of the implications of that speech, or politely stepped past them. She couldn't explain it any better to them than to herself.

"This is the only place I knew of in the entire galaxy where I might be safe, Valentinian," Kyriaki looked hard at the man, willing herself to stillness. "Anyone else might turn me in to the authorities, and they'd put me to death. Same as they would you. I can't go back to my previous life, any more than you two can. Like Dave, I need to find a fresh start."

"Marvelous," Valentinian finally took a third seat and more or less collapsed into it as she watched.

His face suddenly looked Dave's age, drawn and pulled tight over the bones. Those arresting, blue-green eyes were filled with anger, perhaps fighting a touch of despair as she watched.

"Okay," Valentinian finally sighed. "You're here, and in this thing as deep as we are. And that woman won't stop pursuing us, from what both of you have told me. I don't trust you, Kyriaki. I'm not sure I'll ever trust you, but Dave does. Tells me he owes you his life, maybe twice over, so I'm willing to accept that on face value and start with a clear deck right now."

She watched him seem to run out of words. Kind of like she had.

This was what stepping off a cliff felt like, at least until you met water or rocks below. Or, possibly, impossibly, formed wings.

She sipped the spiked coffee and tried to not fidget. Her hands, she knew, were white on the sides of the mug, but it was a metal tough enough she wouldn't leave dents in it, no matter how hard she squeezed right now. She needed that. Something that could hold up to the things in her mind.

"So what's next?" she asked after the companionable silence had begun to stretch and pale.

Dave hadn't moved, but no longer looked like he was measuring her for a shot to center-mass. Much as that might fix most of her problems.

Valentinian eyed her warily from under hooded brows that made him look like a magnificent hawk.

He surprised her by suddenly chuckling.

"Next?" he said with a laugh. "Next is another shell game, only the stakes are much higher this time, if that's possible. And then we're going strange places, lady."

"What's so funny?" she asked.

"I seem to be collecting strays," Valentinian shook his head in mild disbelief. "Dave, you, and probably Bayjy."

He and Dave obviously shared an inside joke and a laugh.

"Who's Bayjy?" Kyriaki asked.

Was there someone else aboard right now? They had only been at this station for barely three days. Was Valentinian expanding his crew?

And why?

"She's the start of the next adventure, Kyriaki," Valentinian replied with another shake of his head. "When things get really weird."

She?

"I see," Kyriaki said diplomatically.

It had not dawned on her that Valentinian might have found himself a girlfriend. Jealousy suddenly reared up and bit her on the ass, on top of everything else, but Kyriaki managed to not flinch. At least she hoped so.

The gleam in Dave's eyes said he saw something Valentinian hopefully hadn't.

But Dave could keep his mouth shut. She already knew that.

[11]
VALENTINIAN

VALENTINIAN HAD DUG out some of his old clothes
and turned them over to the big guy to deliver. His
own cabin was enough for now. He could sit on the
edge of his bunk and just brood. He didn't want to
go upstairs right now and deal with her.

With Kyriaki.

With her implications, or her presence. He hadn't
really stopped thinking about her for the last
however-many-months since she had shown up on
his deck and gotten right into his personal space with
her knowing smile. Fantasies with that face as he lay
down and went to sleep, many nights.

And apparently, from the look in her eyes during
parts of her story, she had the same problem. At least
she had never learned how to play poker with pros.
Couldn't hide all the things in her eyes when the
emotions wanted to dance in the moonlight.

He could pretend he hadn't seen anything. Safer
for everyone, because she still looked like a bounty
hunter right now. Come to collect them for the

reward, regardless of whatever pretty stories the woman might tell.

And Dave…

After they'd put her in cabin three, just off the passenger lounge, he and the big guy had come back downstairs with everything locked up tight, and he had listened to the rest of the story. Not just the tidbits Dave had told him while they had Kyriaki trapped in the forward airlock, but the whole thing.

The Dominator.

Valentinian still wasn't sure how he felt.

On the one hand, mad as hell that he had been so badly manipulated by Dave across the whole process.

On the other hand, the Dominator had had nothing to do with him getting kicked out of Gymnasia Dominia, except to note it on a report somewhere, and file it away against future need. And Dave had explained that he needed someone with a sketchy background, paranoid instincts, and the ability to take care of himself in a tight space. One of the good guys. Someone who could fall into a pile of manure and come out smelling like a rose.

Valentinian already considered that to be his super-power, so he couldn't really argue that last point. With one exception, that had been absolutely the case, and even then, it hadn't turned out all bad. Just bad enough that he wasn't a servant of the old Dominator at that very moment when the man needed an escape.

So they were here. And so was she.

He wasn't sure the galaxy was big enough for all of them. Certainly, Laurentia wasn't, but he had a plan for that.

For the briefest moment, he considered the possibility of dumping both of them, Dave and Kyriaki, at the next station he hit. Wouldn't be all that hard. Might even solve some of his problems.

But he also thought about that asshole that had done the same thing to Bayjy and her crewmates. Abandoned his crew. In that guy's case, greed to collect the whole reward himself, and not have to share it with the others.

Valentinian's excuse wouldn't even be that good. Just fear. Never knowing when the next Dominion assassin would show up, and what they would look like. He could run long and hard and escape everything, if he really wanted to. There were all sorts of places he could go, selling the *Longshot* along the way, stashing the credit, and buying a new identify and a new ship.

Never look back.

Until he remembered just how angry he had been on Bayjy's behalf.

Illegal behavior and unethical frequently overlapped, but not always. That sort of thing was technically legal, depending on the contracts you had, and most spacer's contracts were oral, so almost indefensible in most courts.

That didn't make it right. Wouldn't ever make it right.

He couldn't do that to the two people who were counting on him now.

Three. Maybe five.

Back to Bohrne in a week to see what Bayjy had managed to locate, and talk her down from however mad she would be at his sudden departure. Her second abandonment.

Hopefully the Sheriff would take her aside in all the ruckus and have a quiet, happier conversation with the woman. Same with Stephaneria.

Doing the right thing always seemed to get him deeper in trouble, but hopefully, at least this once, it would work out for the better.

Valentinian stripped off his boots and stretched out on his bunk. She wasn't quite directly above him, but close enough that he could imagine staring at her as she slept, like an angel hovering above him.

Even if she turned out to be the devil in disguise.

[12]
DAVE

DAVE SAT in the galley upstairs and meditated with a pot of tea resting on an electric warming stone.

The kids were both bunked for now. He didn't figure that either of them were actually going to sleep for a while, but they were in their private spaces. He could stay up here in case Kyriaki needed something on an unfamiliar ship, and he was out of Valentinian's hair downstairs.

It had been an interesting conversation, telling Vee the entirety of his last few years. Reliving all the final bits the man would need in order to plan a better escape for everyone.

Dave knew he had spent too much time cooped up inside a bubble of advisors and bodyguards to really plan things quickly on his feet. That was part of the reason Valentinian had been the perfect pick, once Dave had managed to maneuver him into place.

Hopefully, the young man would forgive him, eventually. He had come to like Vee. The Dominion had dealt the kid a bad hand, and he had still managed to work his way through.

Still, Dave could see the man ordering them all off his deck when they got back to Bohrne. High-tailing it for someplace like Lei-Zu where he could get lost in the corporate hustlers and not leave a trail. Show them all his back, for what they had done to him.

Nobody liked to be manipulated or lied to. Of course, there hadn't been any lies. Vee had specifically asked to be a fool rather than an accomplice, back when he only suspected Dave had been an assassin.

Dave laughed to himself and refilled his tea mug. Not that the truth was much better, but at least it was all on the table for now. Tomorrow, they would set out to knit it all back together into a new form.

It helped that Valentinian reminded him of his son Praetextatus. And Kyriaki and Euphrosyne might have seen eye to eye on many things. And he had had to deal with stubborn, opinionated young adults occasionally in over their heads. The children of any given Dominator could choose to stand for a Tournament of Domination, if they wished, but Dave didn't see either of his doing so.

Praetextatus had a good career in front of him as an officer in the Caelons, while his daughter had gone into business and banking. Neither still lived in the palace these days, so they wouldn't have to be evicted. Athanasia could have lived out her days there, had she chosen.

Chasing after him in a Dominion Courier had not been one of the outcomes he had expected or even imagined when he wrote her a letter saying goodbye.

But everybody dealt with grief and rage differently. Or betrayal as she probably saw it.

Kyriaki's door opened and a little light spilled into the corridor from where Dave watched. She emerged a second later and did a double take when she saw him sitting there.

She approached on silent feet, wearing a pair of old socks that one of the girls of Solaria Femina had apparently missed when hurriedly packing, back on Tartarus. Dave's clothes were a little big on her, like Euphrosyne wearing something she had stolen from her father's closet when she was fourteen.

Dave smiled at the memory, and at the young woman before him.

"I couldn't sleep," she said, sliding into the other sofa, across the end table in the middle from him.

"Let me get you a cup and we'll share," Dave said, rising and stepping into the kitchen to unstrap another of the old tea cups.

He couldn't see Valentinian having picked these out, so Dave assumed they came with the ship. Fine porcelain in bone-white with exotic decorations done in blue with a spare hand. They always reminded Dave of a jungle, looking at the images the artist had suggested.

He returned to the lounge to see Kyriaki curled up under one of the quilts that had been stored underneath the pad. For a woman in her mid to late twenties, she looked remarkably like a vulnerable teenager right now. Luckily, he had experience with that kind of creature.

Dave handed her the mug and took his spot. He hadn't been watching anything on the big screen, nor listening to music. Well, the music he was listening to was inside his head, so it probably didn't count.

She filled the cup and sipped. It was just at the perfect temperature and chewiness for Dave, but he had no idea what she preferred,

"Decaf," he said. "Wanted to sleep later."

"I'm not interrupting anything, am I?" her face paled a little.

"No," Dave assured her. "Vee spent about an hour listening to the whole story after you went to bed. He's in his cabin right now, probably about as restless as you are, so I came upstairs for a while, to give him his space."

"And you really are the Dominator?" she asked. "Were?"

"Was," Dave agreed. "And I think I was pretty good at it, but I was done. Just done. However, that's not a job you get to retire from and go live on a beach. Personally, I think they should just have a Tournament of Domination every decade, like clockwork. If the old guy doesn't want to stand, he doesn't have to, and new blood can take over."

"And the Widow?" Kyriaki asked between sips. "What about her?"

"Twenty-five years ago, she was the love of my life, Kyriaki," Dave told her. "But people change. They grow up and sometimes end up different people. She had all the trappings of power and glory, and let it go to her head in bad ways. I suppose I could have divorced her, which probably would have brought out the vultures to challenge me, but I didn't want to fight her anymore. And we had some fantastic fights, over the years. She's smart, stubborn, and opinionated, as you no doubt have learned."

She grimaced at him, but remained otherwise silent.

"So now we can never go back," she said flatly. It wasn't a question, and they both knew it. "How did we get here?"

"Valentinian is good people, Kyriaki," Dave said simply. "That's why I chose him to help make my escape. I had originally hoped we'd get to a certain quiet spot, maybe six months from Dominion Prime, and I could just quit as his first mate and disappear myself. Then you came along."

"And I ruined it for both of you," she said in an angry voice.

"You also tried to do the right thing, young lady," he let his voice grow stern, like he had with another vulnerable fledgling woman he knew. "I would have let you take me in, once you let me rescue Vee. He hadn't asked to be put in that sort of a situation. It was all my fault, everything was my fault, so I was trying to make things right."

"Can we make it right?" she asked, finally turning her attention to look at him, when she had been staring at a space ten thousand light years distant.

"As far as the Dominion is concerned? No," Dave said simply. "Athanasia's the kind who won't let go, and I suspect that the Mandarins of the Solar Party, and whoever will be the new Dominator, would prefer to keep her out here chasing ghosts, rather than have her underfoot where she might cause enough trouble that somebody has to do something about her."

"That's it, then?" her face grew hard. "We turn into pirates and get by outside the law until someone catches up and hangs us from the highest yardarm? That's what we have to look forward to?"

"No, actually," Valentinian's voice suddenly filled the room, causing both of them to start and turn to the kitchen hatch.

Dave had forgotten how quietly Vee could move when he wanted to. Good enough to sneak up on a maudlin, old man tonight, apparently.

Dave grinned at his captain. Vee had apparently walked through some internal fire over the last half hour or so. He looked refreshed in ways that he hadn't in weeks. Not since they first landed on Tartarus.

Dave hoped it was a good sign.

"So where can we go, Captain?" Kyriaki asked in a hot, angry voice. "How can we escape the angry Widow and maybe be safe enough to live more than a few years, constantly looking back over a shoulder for whoever might be gaining?"

Valentinian surprised Kyriaki, but not Dave, by walking over and settling on the couch next to her. Not close enough to touch, not even the quilt over her legs, but still enough in her space to be talking to her, and not just Dave.

"We used to make our living running cargo," Valentinian smiled at her. "But that's too predictable now. Someone will talk and the Widow will eventually discover where to find us, if we make enough friends to have regular runs."

"And now?" Kyriaki asked.

Dave shared Valentinian's grin. So that was where his mind had gone.

"Now, we're getting into the salvage business,"

Valentinian said. "That's one of the reasons we're not actually going to Meskle."

"You're not?" she asked, confused now, which was an improvement over mawkish.

"Nope," Valentinian's smile conveyed true warmth, which gave Dave hope as well. "It'll take them about a week to get to Meskle, and we're running a circle back to Bohrne. When we get there, if she doesn't kill me, Bayjy will have a cargo for us to haul, and Stephaneria will have translated that map for us enough that we can start hunting."

"What map?" Kyriaki's attention was engaged now, so Dave just sipped his tea and laughed inside.

Kids these days.

"I won a treasure map in a crooked poker game," Valentinian beamed at the woman.

"Seriously?" she asked, and then turned his way.

Dave grinned and nodded. He was a witness, after all.

"Who does that?" she continued.

Vee laughed out loud, sounding more like the old captain that had been such a smooth tough-guy at Aestrolathia.

"It's always an adventure out in Wildspace, Kyriaki," Valentinian smirked.

For a moment, Dave was concerned, as her face got serious. Her line earlier about wiping that smug grin off Vee's face. Dave wondered if she might kiss it off, one of these days, but they weren't there. At least not yet. Maybe never.

Kids these days.

"Well, I guess I've signed on to help salvage," Kyriaki said. "Hope the pay's good."

"He'll work you like a dog, Kyriaki," Dave offered. "But he's working harder still. Trust me, I speak from experience."

[13]
VALENTINIAN

BOHRNE STATION WAS WAY DOWN below them, astronomically speaking. Valentinian had specifically brought *Longshot Hypothesis* out of the overdrive well early. Enough so that they would have to bounce back in at some point, or spend the better part of two weeks riding the engines down to the planet. Not worth the headache.

Because he wanted silent darkness today.

Dave was in his starboard seat, looking professional. Kyriaki was standing behind them, just inside the hatch, watching.

"It's beautiful out here," she whispered in a voice probably not meant to be overheard.

Not that there was much space in here. She was almost breathing on his ear as it was.

At least she hadn't thrown a punch at him in the last week. He still wasn't about to let the woman have the passcode to the armory, though. She had Dave to protect her, if she needed something. Or him, technically, he supposed.

Shock pistols didn't do any permanent damage, usually. She might still convince him to experiment. But she had kept her tart tongue to herself, for the most part.

They were all in new territory. How many people got to a place in life where they could never envision being allowed to go home, even if they wanted to?

Valentinian shrugged inside and brought up a system schematic on the main console, setting it to listening. Most of the traffic was one-way transponder. The station broadcasting lane assignments and current vectors of other ships, as you came out of warp and needed to know where to maneuver.

But they were more than two light hours away from the planet, trailing it as it dawdled around the orange-red star in the middle distance.

"Do we trust them?" Dave asked carefully.

"As much as we can anyone," Valentinian grinned back.

They had all had to mentally move to a new place over the last week. Wanted outlaws, damned near anywhere, except maybe here and places the Widow hadn't had a chance to raise an alarm yet.

Valentinian scrolled through the traffic. Bohrne wasn't all that busy a station. Most of the transits were small freighters like *Longshot* passing through with loads of things, plus the occasional mega-transport hauling cargos the size of his ship, to be broken down in orbit and delivered by smaller vessels to specific locations on the planet below.

There. Hopefully, that was the message for him, and not a honeytrap designed lure him in and kill him.

Valentinian had a second course plotted, just in case it was. The benefit of taking the time to drop out of warp this far out. He could set another looping course as a backup and trigger it as soon as he decided he was nervous. This one would be even more fun. It was as exact a reciprocal for Cronus Prime as he could calculate from here.

Someone watching him go would look at his vector and their nav computer would spout apparent gibberish at them. Who returned to the scene of a crime?

Dominion-427, departure outbound on lane 27. Destination Meskle.

Just what it should read, except that it should have been cleared off the boards six days ago, assuming they had chased him into warp the first time. It might still be a trap.

The current list of ships docked at the station didn't include any Dominion-flagged vessels, let alone *Dominion-427*, although that would change if all went well today, adding *Longshot Hypothesis*.

Valentinian hadn't considered that they might have to reflag the *Longshot*. He supposed that made the most sense, at the end of the day. The Dominion wasn't safe for any of them, so they should look for citizenship elsewhere. At least his ship should. The crew had some time before they had to make a decision.

"And?" Dave asked.

"And my paranoia has the better of me," Valentinian admitted. "The evidence suggests that the Widow took the bait. I'm going to drop back into warp for a few seconds, until we get to the normal drop-out point, but I'm ready to run like hell."

"And you think Bayjy will still be there?" Kyriaki asked with an odd tone to her voice.

Valentinian had explained the whole thing to her over the last few days, to prepare her for the fact that the crew might be expanding to four shortly.

"It's not like she had anything pressing when we left," Valentinian said. "Or anywhere to go. I'm really just hoping she's not still mad that we left her."

He engaged the overdrive and blinked through the intervening light hours fast enough he could have held his breath.

Bohrne Station appeared in front of them as their bubble popped and space became a mathematical certainty again. A quick slider on the controls and the autopilot shifted them onto the new heading with the thrusters still off, rolling down and away while still falling forward.

Valentinian sent a hard sensor ping downrange to see as much of the station as he could from here. The locals would have had no idea what direction he might return from, so they wouldn't know what the blind side might be. Plus, they were supposedly broadcasting what he hoped was a complete and accurate list of everybody docked or close by, and none of them were bad guys.

As long as it was truth.

"Bohrne Station, this is *Longshot Hypothesis*, requesting lane assignment for docking," Valentinian sent downrange with a brief prayer.

His hand was still poised on the overdrive button, ready to cast them back into warpspace as fast as the engines could cycle up. He'd sort it out later, if he had to. Just getting gone and surviving would be the important part right now.

"Longshot Hypothesis, this is the Stationmaster," her voice came back. "We'll have a chat about maneuvering rules in my zone, when you land, but Sheriff Bolat-Nurlan says he'll vouch for you. At least for now. Your crew and cargo will meet you on bay seven. Lane assignment transmitted."

Valentinian grinned. They were playing that final hand of Arcades now, and the dealer had just given everybody their seventh card, face down.

The Build card. Time to see if you managed to complete your Arch, or had to bluff into something else.

He spun the ship again, this time dropping ass-first towards the station, and lit the engines to bring them to rest. Hopefully, the reference to crew meant Bayjy, and not the Widow and a crew of gunmen.

He'd burn that bridge when he got there.

BACK TO THE scene of a much-lesser crime, but Kyriaki was still nervous. Technically, boarding *Longshot Hypothesis* in flight had been an act of piracy, something Laurentia took almost as seriously as the Dominion. Valentinian could decide to press charges right now, if he wanted to. It would be a quick and easy way to get rid of her, and there was nothing she could do about it.

Longshot Hypothesis had docked, with a rare, subtle grace and lithe ability that she had come to understand from Dave was uncommon in any other pilot. Most ship-handlers were better off letting the auto-pilot dock something this big with a station, especially backing in and doing the whole thing with cameras, instead of nosing in, like Dominion vessels did, where the airlock was directly in front of your window.

Apparently, Valentinian really was that good.

He turned to her now with an unreadable set of emotions on his face, but Dave got the same look. She almost wondered if he was measuring her for a coffin, but wouldn't say that out loud. At this point, she needed these men probably more than they needed her. And it was his ship.

"Let's go see who's here to welcome us," Valentinian announced as he powered the ship mostly down. Aft, the automated systems were linking them umbilically. Air, water, waste systems were now connected to the station, and recharging.

Kyriaki turned and keyed the cockpit door open, moving into the rec room. Neither man could move until she was out of the way. Valentinian came first, studying her as he walked by, but at least the scowl had receded somewhat. Dave had a big grin for her as he emerged, so she hoped that meant she had at least one ally here.

Valentinian was used to having just one crew member. Artaxerxes until very recently. Now he was looking at having four people on this ship permanently. She wondered how he would react to having to deal with so many humans constantly.

The man struck her as something of an introvert that way. Able to turn his charm on when he needed it, but happy to retreat to his own deck and lock the hatches behind him the rest of the time.

"I had considered sending you out first, while I watched the ship," Valentinian said over his shoulder as he made his way aft. "But I'm not that guy, so I'll go chat with the Sheriff. Dave, you can haul Kyriaki to the chandlery, I've set up credit accounts for both of you on-station, so you can get whatever you need and Kyriaki can get some more clothes. We'll worry about heavier gear once I've had a chance to talk to

Bayjy and get her list of needs, since she doesn't have much more than the clothes on her back, either."

Kyriaki caught the reference to more clothes. Like maybe she could keep the two sets of pants and shirts she had gotten from him plus the Henley. Maybe she had cooties and he didn't want them back afterwards?

She was fine with that. His smell was mostly washed out and covered with hers now, but it had been a pleasant few days. Maybe she'd swap a shirt from his closet when he wasn't looking, just to have the smell again.

She couldn't tell if she was nuts. Or rather, which direction insanity had actually taken her.

They all filed down to the rear airlock and Valentinian called up a deck image of the space beyond. The station had opened they inner bay door, so they could exit anytime they wanted to.

Valentinian had his shock pistol in a thigh holster, like always. Kyriaki suspected he slept with it under his pillow, but wasn't about to say anything. Dave had a matching pistol under his jacket, and that telescoping baton where other people might holster a pistol. And he was probably more dangerous with the stick than the gun.

She was unarmed, beyond her White Hat training in close combat, which was probably sufficient for most situations. Valentinian had told her flat out that he didn't trust her with a gun.

She amended that to *yet* in her head, but really couldn't fault the man. She had chased him clear across the Dominion and almost across Laurentia, intent on doing him some level of harm. So he had not taken the time to key her into the ship's systems. She would need Dave to get back aboard.

The hatch beeped as it slid open towards them. Valentinian went first, then her, then Dave. The welcoming committee was a weird mix, but she could identify all of them, from the stories the two men had shared.

The Sheriff looked exactly like he had been described. Tall and lanky, with short gray hair under a cowboy hat, and a mustache. Keen brown eyes with a delightful humor in them. And a silver badge over his heart as a mark of how important, and dangerous, the man was. Plus a shock pistol of his own. Valentinian had said he had never seen someone who could draw as fast.

The woman standing next to the Sheriff must be his niece, Stephaneria, from the similarity in bones and color. She was taller than Kyriaki by several inches, but probably weighed the same, skinny with almost no curves. She had a warm smile for Valentinian that Kyriaki decided to ignore for now, as she technically had no claim on the man.

The last member of the party awaiting them was probably the most interesting, anyway. Sure enough, layered up to her eyeballs in a heavy jacket, scarf, gloves, knit cap, and hood. All Kyriaki could see was a thin slice of purplish flesh and those black and red eyes.

Bayjy Endon. Supposedly human in form, just executed differently, coming from a *Variant Humanity* that had been engineered for extreme heat. Like Stephaneria, she was tall, but built more like a man, with powerful muscles evident, even under all the layers.

"I'm sorry," Valentinian said out of the blue to Bayjy as they got close. "That's really all I can offer you, at the moment. Things got out of hand and I had to run for my life. But we're back, I'm sorry, and I hope you have good news for us."

Kyriaki was almost as surprised as Bayjy was from the way her eyes got big. She had apparently never expected to hear this hard man go soft and vulnerable like that. It was a side of Valentinian Kyriaki had never expected to see daylight.

Bayjy was rocked back on her heels in a stunned silence. Before she could speak, Valentinian gestured to Kyriaki and addressed himself to the Sheriff.

"So I may have picked up a hitchhiker while I was gone," Valentinian said. "Is that going to be a problem? Kyriaki Apokapes, this is the Sheriff of Bohrne Station."

The Sheriff turned a cold, appraising eye on her now. He just *emanated* cop, a smell she was used to.

"It was my understanding that you had been aboard that other vessel, when it first came in to dock," he said with a tight voice. "How did you come to be with Valentinian, ma'am?"

"If I told you the truth, Sheriff, it would make you an accomplice to everything that happens after this," she replied with a shrug. "Are you sure you wouldn't rather plead ignorance?"

"I'll vouch for her," Valentinian, of all people, said quickly. "And Dave will as well."

"Will you now?" the older man asked with a twinkle in his eyes.

"Yes," Dave said simply. "I owe her my life at least once. Maybe twice. Valentinian as well."

"All right, I'll take that into account," he said,

turning to include all four of them, Bayjy also, as he spoke. "Your friends left in a bit of a huff, so we hopefully have some time to sort things out. Y'all are invited to join me and my niece for dinner in about four hours. And we'll go from there. Valentinian, you have a meeting with the Stationmaster to get yelled at in about an hour, so expect an angry woman, but the fines won't be all that bad."

"Yes, sir," Valentinian replied.

Valentinian turned to her now with a grim smile.

"I might be a while, but we should be ready to run like hell anyway," he said. "I'll work with Bayjy now and then the Stationmaster. You two go shop and we'll meet back here in a few hours and plan for dinner, assuming *Dominion-427* doesn't drop out of warp on us right away."

"If they do, we'll treat them like pirates for now," the Sheriff surprised her by saying. "This isn't the Dominion, and they claim diplomatic privilege. That cuts both ways around here, especially if they threaten a neutral cargo transport on my dock."

Kyriaki shivered at the cold tone in the man's voice. But he was right. Even the Widow wouldn't dare provoke the Laurentian government by herself. If she was smart, she'd ditch the courier at some point and hire herself a proper privateer. Plausible deniability.

They weren't unheard of, but the penalties for piracy were the same. It would, however, give the woman more leeway to chase them.

Kyriaki felt eyes on her. She turned to see Bayjy scoping her hard, eyes squinted. Bundled up like that, it was impossible to see the rest of her face, but the eyes were intense.

Kyriaki's chin came up, just a bit. Challenging, but not threatening.

If you want to play games of pack dominance, I'll show you a few things, lady. *Variant Humanity* or not. I've taken down men bigger than you by myself.

Kyriaki packaged that into a serene smile and wafted it back at the woman. The message seemed to be understood, because the eyes grew a little friendlier. The other woman, the niece, wasn't quite so friendly, but there was nothing Kyriaki could do about that.

She glanced up at Dave, apparently watching everything with a silent grin, like he did. A man who thought before he acted.

"Shall we?" she asked politely.

Dave nodded and turned to the right, those long legs setting a pretty good clip that she had to stride hard to keep up with. At least it got them away from the rest of the setting quickly enough.

"Is this going to work?" she asked him quietly, in a very different voice, as they got far enough around the curve of the station that the others started to fade from sight.

"Maybe," Dave offered.

That's what she liked about the man. If he wasn't certain, he wouldn't lie about it. And if he was unsure, then maybe the rest of them were, as well.

Fifteen minutes' walk on a largely empty promenade brought the two of them to the more commercial district, past the bars and the food court. Dave had apparently been here previously, as he walked right to a particular shop and entered the space. A bell chimed as they entered.

Without a card-reader, Kyriaki was almost a nonperson, but Dave assured her that they would have her picture and vital stats on record. Just in case, she sought out the woman behind the counter.

"Good morning," Kyriaki said. "I am currently recovering from losing everything in a crash and don't have a card-reader or identity papers. My captain should have entered me into the station database? Kyriaki Apokapes."

"Can you spell that?" she asked, so Kyriaki did. "Ah, here you are."

She spun the screen around to show the picture of her that Valentinian had taken on his cargo deck, wearing his clothes. The credit amount next to it nearly made her goggle, but she controlled herself, assuming that she would be working that off as debt going forward.

"Thank you," she said, leading Dave deeper into the store and to the left, where a nice selection of women's clothing was to be found.

After five minutes, she moved over to the men's section, looking for pants with pockets big enough to be more than decorative. She had a package of four gray or black t-shirts that wouldn't be too tight across her chest, but still fit well enough to show off her muscles a little. None of the pants over there would work, that was certain. Too much emphasis on being girlie, apparently.

She wondered if all female spacers out here had to go someplace special for that, or just wore men's clothing. Or maybe just didn't go into space in the first place. Stephaneria, meeting them at the dock, had worn a long skirt, clear down to her ankles and flowing. It looked nice, but would never fit into a suit.

Granted, the most you were supposed to wear in a full suit was a T-shirt, with everything else plugged into plumbing of some sort, but still.

The only thing she didn't bother with was a package of brassieres. She was in good enough shape to not need them now, and not big enough that she needed the support.

Gray-green pants, three of. Undershirts, one package. Hooded sweatshirt with kangaroo pouch. Two blue Henleys and a button-up flannel in red and black. Socks. Panties. Gloves. Knit cap.

Enough to get her by for several days at a time, provided she did laundry on a regular basis. And the machines were on her deck upstairs, so it wasn't as long a walk as it was for the boys.

And she had used only about a third of the money Valentinian had advanced, so she looked for other things.

"Am I allowed a weapon?" she asked Dave as they departed the store, two big bags in her hands.

Dave shrugged.

"As long as it's a knife or baton, probably," he said. "Vee's still a little nervous around you, so I wouldn't push it on a beam, just yet."

"What's his dysfunction?" she asked with a little more snarl than she probably intended to sound.

"If I had to guess, he still sees you as a cop, Kyriaki," Dave said quietly. "A White Hat. And he's had some bad experiences with that kind that he needs to get over. Plus, I've got a head start on coming to grips with you over him."

She kept her grumbles to herself.

"I will remind you," Dave continued in a voice low enough she had to lean in against him to hear as they walked. "You could still kill us both and concoct any story you wanted for the Widow. They might even buy it, without anybody else to gainsay you."

"You know that's bullshit, Dave," she barked back.

"I know that, Kyriaki," he said to her. "Vee's still got to process that internally. Once we're well and gone beyond anything the Widow can do, I expect he'll calm down some."

What was worse was that Dave was right. She was an alien here. A renegade cop already so far past recovery that there was nowhere to go but forward.

Hopefully, Valentinian would understand that at some point.

Even if she did decide to kill them both and haul a pair of heads back to the Dominion, she had no doubts that the first thing someone would order was to put her to questioning under truth serum, from which she would probably never awaken, once her own crimes came out.

How did she explain that to the man? Wait, she supposed, until he came around to it himself.

There was nothing more she could do right now, except pay him back for the loan, and start carving herself a place on the other side of the law.

VALENTINIAN WATCHED Dave lead Kyriaki away to get new clothes. As he turned back, Bayjy was eyeballing him. It looked like she was grinning inside that scarf, but he didn't feel like asking. It was still too complicated for an outsider, and Bayjy still was.

The Sheriff and Stephaneria extracted a promise of dinner and gave him the address, before walking off. Stephaneria left him with an extra warm smile first, though. Then he was left with Bayjy and her damnable smile.

"I accept," the woman said.

It took him a moment to process her words. She was accepting his apology, hopefully.

He nodded, grateful.

"I had a long, rather angry conversation with the Sheriff after you left," she continued. "He actually came and found me. Told me part of what was going on. At least the boring, public bits. Still looking forward to hearing the rest. Already figure I'll be an accomplice, since I plan to be sailing with you."

Valentinian sighed.

"Not in public," he promised, starting to move off back to the ship for now. There wasn't much traffic on the promenade, but enough. "Even here, there will be ears. Were you able to score me a cargo going somewhere?"

"Yes, depending," she said, following.

Once they were both aboard, Valentinian sealed the hatch back up for now and led her into the larger cargo bay. The forward hatches were all sealed up and would stay that way.

"Talk to me," Valentinian turned to her with a grim smile.

"So the planet exports tropical fruit," Bayjy said. "The whole equatorial band down there is pretty much island paradise for people like you."

"Like me?" he was lost.

"Eighteen degrees in the winter, maybe twenty-seven at the peak of a summer day," her eyes grinned at him. "You wanna impress me, take me to a desert planet somewhere."

"Oh, right," Valentinian nodded. Too cold for her. A little too warm for him, most seasons.

Given his preference, Valentinian would have settled in an alpine zone somewhere, a valley that only got maybe a meter of snow in the winter, and barely melted it off by the end of summer. But he knew most people thought that was weird.

"So I talked to the Sheriff, and he talked to some people," Bayjy continued, her smile evident in her voice. "You apparently impressed the hell out of the right people, because they offered us three different deals. First: they pay us straight FOB to haul a load of tropical fruit and stuff to Begzatlari. Second: we go halves on costs up front and take half on the back. Third: we buy as much as we can carry at a damned nice rate that looks like about a ten percent discount, and do whatever we want with it at the other end."

"What's the best, in terms of long-term storage refrigerated?" Valentinian asked. "I can stow boxes in here and turn the temperature down to just above freezing, but we have a different problem long term."

"I presumed that, from the way you had to light out," her voice got more serious. "The Dominion's after you?"

"They were after Dave," he said. "But now it will be expanded to me. Once they know you and Kyriaki are aboard, they'll come after you as well."

"That bad?" she asked.

"Let's just say that I have no intention of ever letting them take me alive," he felt his face grow hard and fierce. "What they would do to any of us is worse than death. That's what you're signing up for, as well, because they'll torture you for information you won't have until we trust you more."

"And how long's that going to be?" she got sharp. "If I'm signing up for death, I deserve to know why."

"I'll make you a deal," he leaned forward just a little. "We finish our first run successfully, and I'll let Dave tell you. More fun that way."

"Wow," he finally heard doubt creep into her voice.

This woman was an unbridled optimist, as near as he could tell. It would be nice to dent that.

Valentinian shrugged.

"Kyriaki used to be a White Hat before this," he said. "That's the Dominion's Internal Security troops. And she's a wanted outlaw with the rest of us now."

"Shit," Bayjy's voice got small. "You people are intense."

"I am serious," Valentinian said. "And you deserve to know that much before you sign on. I'll let you back out right now with no hard feelings. But once we make this first run, we have to disappear."

"Why?"

"Because if we start running a circuit, if someone has an idea where to find us, there will be gunships on our flank one of these days," Valentinian said. "This cargo is to get us some cash and some distance. Maybe it buys us some gear for you and Dave, since I'm pretty sure my one armored cargo-lifter might not fit you across the chest, and is way too short for Dave. Right now, the only thing between me and a life of piracy is that map from the poker game."

"Damn, Valentinian," she said, voice all happy and snarky again. "You sure know how to show a girl a good time."

Valentinian smiled at the joke. Anything from here wasn't going to be solely his fault. He had warned her. If she chose to ignore those warnings, there wasn't much he could do about it.

And he knew she was getting desperate. Not much in the way of jobs on this station, and that would eventually mean she had to drop down to the surface and find something, where the odds of her getting back into space would get worse every day.

He'd been there. But for luck and a crooked poker game…

"Okay," he said. "So let's go talk to your dealers about prices and cargo. I've got a little while before the Stationmaster rips me a new one, and then a complicated dinner with the Sheriff, where we have to keep him mostly in the dark while staying on his good side. Hopefully, his niece was able to narrow our map down some, so we know where we're going after all this."

"And if she doesn't?" Bayjy followed as he started towards the airlock.

"Then we'll have to keep trying, getting progressively deeper into Wildspace, Bayjy," he said. "I don't think we can even stay in Laurentia longer than absolutely necessary, to say nothing of coming back. Maybe we'll go visit your homeworld."

"I don't have a homeworld, Valentinian," she said starkly. "My kind are wanderers, born on stations and ships. The Urlan homeworld where they originally created us was one of the ones destroyed during the war."

"Then you'll fit right in with the rest of us," he gave her a grim smile. "None of us are ever going home, either."

VALENTINIAN

IT HADN'T TURNED out too bad. Not near as loud and angry as Valentinian had expected. The Stationmaster sat him down, handed him a list of moving violations with fines attached and then suspended ninety-five percent of them if he could keep from racking up any more trouble in the next fourteen months.

From the wicked smile in her eyes, she had known the chances of him coming back to Bohrne station in the next year were almost zero, so she was apparently writing it off. He had paid her cash out of his pocket on the remaining five percent, promised to be a good boy, and gotten sent home with a brand new, plas-paper pamphlet of the piloting regulations for this station.

Probably a collector's item she had printed specifically to hand him as a reminder.

Now the fun part.

They were back at that steak house. Back in that same room where he had first taken Bayjy to talk business. Apparently, the room was specifically configured to handle *Variant Humanity*. He must have missed that the first time.

Tonight, everyone was in their lightest clothing. For Valentinian, a simple T-shirt and his usual pants and boots. And the gun. Dave was in something similar. Even Kyriaki had gotten in the act.

Sitting across from him, he found her distracting. A light shirt, more or less skin tight across the chest with nothing under it, did that to him.

The Sheriff was in a simple button-up shirt, and Stephaneria was in silks that seemed cool enough. Not as sheer as Kyriaki's and she seemed to be regretting that choice, but Valentinian kept his opinions to himself.

Bayjy was in heaven. That much was obvious. She was all the way down to a heavy Henley, not even bringing her gloves or hat since it was around forty in here. At the same time, the folks at the restaurant had dug out of storage the niftiest piece of kit Valentinian had ever seen. He would be stealing the idea shortly.

The chairs plugged into the floor, and had a local temperature setting. The air around him might be intolerable, but his butt was nicely chilled and that kept the rest of him pleasantly adjusted. He had figured he could get a butt warmer for Bayjy, but this was a small slice of heaven for him, as well.

He presumed her butt warmer was cranked up as high as it would go.

Weird, but it worked.

The fruit salad appetizer had been delightful. The steaks had been fantastic. Small talk about this and that, without ever addressing the dangerous bits, had been charming.

Now they were down to the hard points. The Sheriff set his coffee mug down and speared Valentinian with a hard look.

"Before *Dominion-427* left, they filed a fugitive warrant for your first mate," he said in a calm, straightforward voice. "Accused him of being an assassin, while not getting too deep into the details of who he is accused of killing. Thoughts, young man?"

Valentinian set his own coffee down. He hadn't been dreading this moment, so much as preparing mentally for it all day.

"So when I first hired Dave, he saved me from getting my ass kicked by five thugs and their pimp," Valentinian's smile had no more warmth than the Sheriff's. "Later, there was a suggestion of certain things. You want to know what I told him?"

"Sure," the older man nodded, a ghost of a smile as he recognized the storytelling elements.

"I told Dave I'd rather be an ignorant fool, if they ever caught us," Valentinian smiled, glancing over at Bayjy and seeing how intently she was following things. "I didn't actually get the honest truth from the man until we were outbound from this station a week ago, and only then because I had Kyriaki standing in my forward airlock asking to come in from the cold. And *only then* because the two of them required that I know, in order to plan what our next steps had to be."

"I see," the Sheriff's grin turned a mite frosty now. "So you're suggesting that I don't want to know?"

Valentinian shrugged.

"You are an Officer of the Courts, Sheriff," Valentinian said. "That warrant is technically a legal document, and if you spent the time to get clarification from a Dominion representative, they would probably validate it."

"Would they now?" the man asked. "And you believe I might choose to ignore it, if I did know the whole story?"

"If you did, it would make you a target as well," Kyriaki spoke up now, from her spot on the man's immediate right. "I speak from experience, since I used to be a White Hat. Someone would send people after you, if for nothing more than to put you under a truth serum to find out what you knew. And then they would kill you for knowing this. Even that badge won't protect you."

Valentinian liked the sidelong look she got for that. He didn't trust her, not yet, but she was trying. He had to give her that.

"Oh, and they will be back here, once they realize we never made it Meskle, Sheriff," Dave chimed in. "I'm intimately familiar with the woman in command of that vessel. Tenacious only begins to describe her."

"So y'all think you have it all figured out?" he asked coldly, leaning forward enough to rest his elbows on the table and his chin on his hands.

"Oh, hell no, Sheriff," Valentinian laughed. "But hindsight is an exact science. I know every decision that got us here, and I wouldn't change any of them. Tomorrow's the dangerous part."

Out of the corner of his eye, even Kyriaki flinched a little, like she had been expecting to be one of those things he considered a mistake. But seriously, she had saved his life at least twice, so far, maybe three times, depending on how you wanted to count it.

It was that hungry expression she occasionally got in her eyes, when she didn't think anyone was looking, that left him just a few degrees off true.

The Sheriff turned to Dave now, with an appraising eye.

"You did say *intimate*, Mr. Hall?" he asked. "I heard you correctly?"

Dave shrugged with a slight grin.

"That's where I think you might be wandering out onto the thinner ice, sir," Dave replied, almost cordially.

"Uh huh," the grin came back. "There was an interesting accusation, Hall, accompanying the warrant."

"I might challenge someone to produce a body," Dave's grin back turned cold and savage. "That is, if we were to somehow end up in a Court of Law instead of a firefight."

Valentinian held his breath while the Sheriff turned and stared at Kyriaki. Her chin came up, but she remained silent. Then the older man turned his direction.

Valentinian felt like he was back across the poker table from the man, knowing in his soul that the Sheriff had just drawn a Perfect Granite Arcade with his Build card. The best hand possible.

"I see," he said, almost to himself, but his eyes were on Valentinian. "Son, you might be playing the most dangerous game I have ever even known, but I'll give you credit for audacity and as much honesty as this situation allows you. Hopefully, your Dominion friend won't decide to start a war here. As you said, I don't know the truth, unless she deigns to tell me later, but this is Laurentia, not the Dominion.

And I'm just an old country Sheriff, easily bamboozled by you city folk. I'll leave all that complicated stuff to the diplomats."

Valentinian felt a deep sigh escape his soul. From the way the others around the table slumped in unison, they had also been holding their breath, waiting.

The Sheriff grinned. It was a thing of bright, honest joy on his weathered face. He turned to his niece on the other side.

"So I understand that Valentinian won a treasure map in a poker game," he exclaimed with the innocence of driven snow.

Stephaneria only slightly rolled her eyes at the man. After all, it was his crooked poker game that caused all this in the first place. And everyone here knew it.

She smiled at Valentinian as if they had an inside joke about her uncle's behavior.

"So I was able to get what I think was a match for the map," she began in a careful, deliberate voice.

"That's wonderful," Valentinian couldn't contain himself. "How?"

"It turns out that most of the stars were simply marked with color and an approximate distance from the central one," she smiled like a detective with *one more thing*. "But two of them were actually annotated in Urlan, listing the star names themselves. The map itself looked relatively new, but the information inscribed on it dates back at least two thousand years, based on variable drift, once I knew where to look."

"So back to the war?" Bayjy asked, voice alive with equal amounts of hope and avarice.

Valentinian watched the lavender woman, seeing her face for the first time tonight. She was attractive, if heavy-boned. And completely bald, which was weird. And purple instead of his pink. But still human. Still a woman.

Utterly irrepressible.

"It looks like," Stephaneria replied. "I can't be sure, because Valentinian kept a portion of the map secret when I scanned the rest. I think I can get you as close as the right star, and presumably that other column of numbers gets you to the target itself, if it's still there after all this time."

"It does," Valentinian agreed. "Something put into orbit of one of the moons of one of the planets, so presumably safe, assuming they dropped it into a LaGrange point where it was stable. What do I owe you for your time?"

She fixed him with a strange look. Unreadable. Calculating.

"The money I gave you was just an opener, a retainer, Stephaneria," he continued. "I'm sure you did more work than that, especially if you had to translate Urlan."

"Pictures of whatever it is," she finally said, after a long, wistful look he really didn't want to try to decipher.

"That might be a while," he said carefully. "We're going to be wanted fugitives pretty soon. No place in Laurentia is likely to be officially safe."

"Then you should make sure your transponder doesn't say *Longshot Hypothesis* when you return, Valentinian," the Sheriff got serious now.

That was about as good an invitation as he was likely to ever get, all things considered.

"I'm not going to win this one, am I?" he asked them both.

Stephaneria smiled.

"Stubborn doesn't run anywhere in the family, Valentinian," she said, nodding to her uncle.

The older man just nodded.

"In that case, I would be much obliged if you sent the data over, first chance you got, and told me what section of the galactic navigational charts I needed to purchase," Valentinian said.

He looked around and decided he was done, so he slid his chair back.

"Thank all of you for a lovely dinner and conversation," he said, turning to his crew. "I'll see the rest of you in the morning, bright and early, and we'll see about taking on cargo."

"Where are you going?" Dave asked, confused.

"Down to the clinic to get my medical records updated," Valentinian said.

The others hadn't stirred much as he rose and moved to the door.

The Sheriff had a surprised look on his face, glancing right and left at the two women seated to either side before meeting Valentinian's eyes with a hint of disbelief. The others were slower on the uptake, but they weren't spacers yet. Bayjy was the closest, but she was more of a salvager. Still, she caught on second after the Sheriff, fixing him with a good case of stinkeye as he opened the hatch and nodded to her and the Sheriff.

It was an old euphemism among spacers. You had to go to the clinic first, to get checked out and get all your immunizations updated, so that your next stop could be the cathouse a few doors down. Had to make sure you were healthy and not bringing anything aboard that you might leave behind.

After all, the working girls and boys in the whorehouse got checked up monthly as part of their employment.

Valentinian was pretty sure he might have gotten as many as three offers to help what troubled him, just in that dining hall alone, had he broached the subject informally. And they were all pretty women, without a doubt.

And not one of them—Kyriaki, Stephaneria, nor Bayjy—was worth the grief that might come along with it tomorrow.

Tonight, he would rely on the tender, loving care of an impersonal professional.

[17]
BAYJY

BACK IN SPACE AGAIN. Finally. Thank the gods. Through the hatchway, she could even see warpspace out the front windshield over Captain's shoulder.

Bayjy had held serious reservations about ever getting onto a ship again, after that bastard Butler had dumped her and everybody else on Bohrne. But for some serious fast talking with Valentinian, and the luck of a poker game she really shouldn't have been in in the first place, she'd have been in deep trouble. The kind that left you looking down at the possibility of harvesting pineapples for a living pretty damned quick.

Of course, there were a lot of pineapples and coconuts in her future, anyway. About six hundred cubic meters of each, stacked up in wooden shipping crates that pretty much filled the cargo bay of *Longshot Hypothesis*.

It was fun, listening to the rest of them bitch about the cold, since the Captain had brought the permanent temperature in there down to just a few degrees above water freezing. Bayjy could barely tell the difference from what they considered pleasant stuff.

And Captain had been right about her wearing his cargolifter. If she didn't have breasts, it would have been uncomfortable but doable, since her shoulders and lats were about the same circumference as his. Too much painful squish in front to handle for more than a few minutes.

She would need to save up enough cash to buy her own. Maybe ask Captain to front her a loan with good rates, since she had gotten him a fantastic deal on fresh fruit transport. Hall would be in the same boat, since nobody carried gear for a human that size.

They didn't come that size, out in Wildspace. Urlans, sure, frequently. M'Rai were even bigger, but most of *Variant Humanity* was not that man's size.

So she was in the rec room forward right now. Begzatlari was coming up in a little while, once they dropped out of the bubble and backed up against the station. She had a letter of introduction from folks back on Bohrne, for folks here, and a crap-ton of fruit to deliver.

And *Longshot Hypothesis* really was as fast as Captain refused to admit. The fruit was getting here two days faster than even *Hard Bargain* might have been able to deliver it, let alone your standard transport.

Fresh *fresh* fruit sold for way more, since you had more options about using it, the more days until it went bad.

Money money money.

"So what was it you did, as a salvager?" Kyriaki's

voice brought Bayjy back from dreams of swimming in pools of gold coins, like a fantasy dragon.

"Huh?" Bayjy managed eloquently.

"What were your tasks, on a wreck?" Kyriaki asked.

The human chick was seated across from her. They both had a good view of the bridge, but that cockpit was too small for all four of them, and Captain and Hall were flying the ship.

"Partly, I was muscle for some of the smaller crew," Bayjy replied. "But I was also a Senior Cutter, so I'd go into some tight places to get something loose with either a cutting laser or the diamond saw."

"Why not just repair a ship and fly it home?" Kyriaki asked, her face all scrunched up with concentration.

"Most of what you'd ever find was in too bad a shape to ever repair," Bayjy smiled. "And that sort of work's expensive, when ships tend to be pretty cheap. You'd have to have something enormously valuable to be worth it. Lots of half-dead ships sitting in salvage yards in orbit or down on a planet."

"Huh," the ex-cop grunted. "So you go in and gut it for a quick profit?"

"Pretty much," Bayjy said with pride. "Every day in space costs you something, even if just fuel and food for the crew. Gear gets worn out. Margins are razor thin, most of the time. And then you occasionally run into an Urlan Troop Transport with the forward section still in miraculous shape, even though the aft had been shot to shit."

"That was the ship your old captain looted, before Bohrne?"

"Yup," Bayjy forced the smile to stay put, as much

as it wanted to wander off somewhere else. "That time, we took whole wall sections out on weld seams, so that it could be reassembled later with some tack welds and be good. And we had all the religious paraphernalia to go with the icons, so somebody would pay good money for it, either an Urlan church or a collector with a weird fetish."

"Fetish?" Kyriaki's face turned all the way around to stare at her now, instead of the back of Captain's head.

"The Urlan created my kind as a slave species from your kind, Kyriaki," Bayjy noted dryly. She let the smile wane a little, but not so far as angry. "There are some sick weirdoes out there, obsessively collecting odd bits for reasons I'd rather not contemplate."

"Gotcha," the cop nodded. Ex-cop. She still walked like a cop, but seemed to be getting better.

They lapsed into silence as the Overdrive receded. Most people couldn't tell, but Bayjy had always had an eighth sense for that sort of thing on a ship.

Hallelujah, they had made it to Begzatlari. Time to get out of the delivery business, and into some serious fun.

"Hey, Bayjy," Captain asked over his shoulder. "Can I make your day, if you promise to behave?"

Behave? She'd seen the looks he'd given her, when she was down to just a few layers, and those were a little tight. Or when he watched her try out the cargo lifter in the buff. She wasn't sure when *he* was going to break down and misbehave, but she also didn't know when Kyriaki might finally break out of her shyness and pin the guy to a bulkhead for a good smooching.

Hall was a little too old for her tastes, but ya never knew. He might be a good romp, if she got desperate.

"Maybe," she called back ambiguously. "Girl like me's not always known for decorum, so's you know."

Both men laughed up in the cockpit. That was part of the problem, the pink-skins were all a little too wrapped up tight. Fortunately, Captain had done something about it at Bohrne, although she'd been flat out surprised he hadn't asked that librarian. The librarian had looked pretty surprised, too.

The other two should have taken care of it, as well, but that was their business.

She'd been too broke to rent help. And afraid she might break a mere human if she got a little carried away in throes of a really good, pent up orgasm.

"So I got a list of current vessels docked at the station," Captain said in a voice that sounded positively evil.

Something about it had her butt out of the chair with the heater in the seat and standing in the hatchway. She drifted a little too close to Captain's ear when Kyriaki came up behind her. He flinched as she breathed on him but it wasn't like she was going to bite him or anything.

At least not without an invitation.

Not yet, anyway.

"What bright and exciting news do you think will cause me to *misbehave*, Captain?" she murmured in as sultry a voice as she could manage, chuckling inside.

He leaned a little forward so he could turn to look back at her without them actually kissing.

"Docked in port nine," he smiled. "Someone you might recognize. Thought you should know."

She looked over his shoulder at the board in the center. And lit a blue streak a mile and a half-wide.

That low-down, double-dealing, no-good, snake in the grass. Here? I'll murder him.

"No," Captain said in a harder voice than she thought the boy even knew.

And apparently she had forgotten to use her inside voice today, because Hall was looking at both of them like maybe he was about to be in the middle of something he'd rather just watch from the safety of a good telescope.

Bayjy let the smile turn kinda snarly at her captain. He was the reason she wasn't picking coconuts for a living.

"No?" she asked, about as friendly as was possible, considering that *Hard Bargain* was just across the way, innocent as mud and everything.

"No," Captain said firmly. "I know what you'd like to do to the man, and I agree with it, pretty much bowsprit to stern. However, I have a better idea. *Meaner.*"

She liked the way the man enunciated that last word. The emphasis on a promise of ugly pain for Butler. She could listen to a better idea than just grabbing a hunk of pipe and knocking politely on Butler's forward hatch.

"But you gotta behave first," Captain continued in that hard-as-freaking-nails-killer voice she had just discovered the man had. "Understand?"

That might just excite her more, if the kid was that dangerous on top of being that cute. She might have to pin him to a wall for some groping herself, before Kyriaki worked up the courage to do it.

"All right," she huffed, just a little.

So he told her. And she laughed and laughed and laughed.

Yeah, she could behave for something like that, especially if they could somehow pull it off. Captain was even meaner and sneakier than she had imagined. Hall and Kyriaki seemed content with Captain's idea, too.

Oh, Butler, if you weren't such a son of a bitch, I might even feel sorry for you.

But you got this coming.

[18]
DAVE

Dave had never met an Urlan before. Hell, until Bohrne, he'd never even heard of the species, but ancient history had never been his thing and they had happened a long time ago and way the hell across space.

Plus, their ancient empire had been sacked, burned, and salted two thousand or more years ago. These days, they were just another species you might encounter in deep space. At least this far out.

Big, though. His size, when he was used to being about a hand taller than even most of his Caelons had been, and half a head taller than his civilian advisors. Maybe weighed as much, too, if he were to run into one that was a warrior instead of a shopkeeper, like this guy.

Dark brown skin, even swarthier than his best tan ever got. Black eyes hard and piercing.

They weren't one of the *Variant Humanities*, but had hit on a convergent evolution that put them close enough that they could pass, with a little work. The

142

only big difference were the head ridges. They started as heavy scales just below the widow's peak and went back like a line of rounded spikes clear to the back of the skull, with a two patches of straight, black hair just above and behind the ears, like an old, half-bald human, except for the scales that kept going to the neck.

From what he had looked up in a moment of curiosity, there were similar scale-like things protecting the shoulders, upper chest, and most of the back, as well as bits on the elbows and knees. It was almost like they had evolved with armor, where humans just had skin and nails at the ends of their digits. And the material was only a little tougher than his fingernails, but that little bit was frequently sufficient, if you ran into a predator with teeth.

These days, knives wouldn't turn much, but again, every little bit helped.

The shopkeeper was lanky. Dave's height and maybe two or three stone lighter. A touch defensive, but that might come from being the only one of his kind, and living on the wrong side of Wildspace from the rest of his species.

Dave wondered if this was another one who could never go home.

But clothing in here just magically happened to run more in his size than most chandlery shops, so Dave could find things that fit him. Pants that he didn't have to tuck into tall boots because they were plus-fours on him. Shirts that came all the way down to his wrists.

"Are you seeking to fulfill specific needs?" the shopkeeper was suddenly close by.

Dave had heard him moving around, but hadn't

realized he was coming to chat. The look wasn't necessarily friendly, but wasn't all the hostile, either.

"I'm new in this sector," Dave said, gesturing to the racks and piles around him. "Finding clothing that fits comfortably without tailoring is frequently difficult. I live in dread of being unable to find a cargo liftersuit that fits me."

"Ah," the man nodded. He stepped close and a tape measure was suddenly present in his hands like a magic trick. "If you would stand perfectly still for a moment, let me take your dimensions."

Dave did so, watching like a hawk as the man went about his work. The only term Dave could think of was fussy. And apparently professional, as he held all the numbers in his head until he was done, before retiring to his counter and writing them down from memory.

Dave followed.

"They are nearly impossible to find around here," the shopkeeper said. "However, your dimensions are such that an Urlan suit in size medium would almost be a perfect fit. If you go deeper into Wildspace, and perhaps outward from the Core in a clockwise motion, you might have some luck."

Medium? That suggested a Large or Extra Large. Good to know.

"What name should I attach to the measurements, in case you need to order more gear on a future trip?" he continued

Dave nearly gave his name, before he stopped himself. Even innocently, he should leave no trail here.

"Demetrios," he replied carefully.

The Urlan shopkeeper smiled knowingly and

wrote it at the top of the page. Then he surprised Dave by making an exact copy from memory and handing it to him.

"When you next encounter a professional tailor, or return at a later date, this will need to be updated, but it will give them a significant starting point," he said. "Now, how else can I be of assistance?"

Dave ended up with three new outfits, paying cash in Solars he had quietly withdrawn back on Tartarus before they left. Back when Dave knew that the hunters would be coming, and he had to close the bank account to thwart them, even a little. There were still others he could tap.

And Vee probably had no idea how much money Dave had stashed in his cabin. He could have purchased that entire load of fruit and had funds left over, but Valentinian was extremely careful with his money. By only putting up half, Vee had also guaranteed that the sellers would give them the best stock to transport, since they had to front the other half of the money and would want the best profit they could manage at this end.

And Dave now knew someone here that might be able to find him gear that fit. He nodded to the man as he left, bags in hand and an honest smile on his face for the first time in weeks.

HE KNEW IT WAS UNFAIR, but Valentinian had been absolutely adamant that Bayjy couldn't leave the ship when they docked. Too much risk of her, or a memory of her, making it to the M'Rai captain. This game wouldn't work if the man had the slightest warning.

Instead, he was out scouting the station himself. And Kyriaki had gotten measurements and details necessary to purchase things for Bayjy. She could at least bring gender experience to the table. Valentinian would be clueless, except to go in with whatever exact list the Pranai woman provided and hope that he could get a match.

Plus, it got everyone out of everyone's hair for a while. Dave was off shopping. Kyriaki as well, but in different places. And the soon-to-be-notorious Captain Tarasicodissa was in a bar. The adventure had kind of started in a bar. Two of them. And a library, depending on how you wanted to spin it.

Hopefully, it would end in a bar, and not someplace worse.

This place was about in the middle on a roughness scale, as station joints went. Not the high end bar and restaurant where the rich spacers hung out, but not the place where the dregs and the cheapest crew sucked down the thinnest beers they could afford, either.

For Valentinian, just a chance to scout things. Before now, he had never even left the Dominion in his travels. It was only here that he truly began to realize what a specist place his old home was. And within that, racist as well.

Laurentia didn't care what shape or color you were, as long as you had money and behaved. He had seen regular humans with skin that was almost golden, or a brown so deep it was almost red, or a different brown verging over into charcoal black itself. His kind were pink by comparison, but referred to as white universally. And not always necessarily in a friendly way.

But there were many *Variant Humanities* out here. No other Pranai, like Bayjy, but Daicia, and Jynarri. And he had even seen a Viddhu out on the concourse, meter and a half tall and probably heavier and stronger than him, originally engineered for mining in tight quarters, because the Urlan in those days would rather have played at being gods with their genetic engineering than to just strip the top of a mountain off with heavy machinery to get at the seams of valuable metals underneath.

The M'Rai were another Variant Humanity, but one fairly uncommon in Laurentia. Or anywhere even this half of Wildspace, to hear Bayjy explain it.

Captain Vidy-Wooders's kind were still far wanderers, though, almost Vikings in the way their ships covered all of Wildspace and the various star nations that fronted on that open, dangerous zone.

Valentinian had tracked the man, whom Bayjy called Butler with a growl in her voice, to this bar. A word here, a coin there. Perhaps the suggestion of a clandestine meeting that needed to happen, and people had pointed him here.

Valentinian didn't approach the man today. Just stood, more or less leaned against one end of the bar where he could watch. He hadn't asked anyone any questions about the man, just suggestions as to where to find him.

Butler Vidy-Wooders. M'Rai. Three meters tall, from the looks of him. Not quite built like Dave, but still strong. Long brownish-blond hair pulled into a rough ponytail with a leather clamp. Full beard kept reasonably trimmed but starting to show white on both sides of the chin.

The species had been engineered by the Urlan as warriors, once upon a time, men and women with muscles enough to handle any of their other servant species or *Variant Humanity* alone.

The man had a huge laugh, to go with his enormous size. And a matching appetite, to see the steak delivered to him. It looked like a kilogram of meat, two fingers thick and as big around as the plate, with vegetables and potatoes and rolls served separately.

Didn't appear to be his first trip to this station either, as he had a pitcher of beer and a stein to drink from that were both built to his scale.

The man was here alone, would be Valentinian's

guess. Seated at a long, communal table with a couple of local merchants nearby, but not *with* him. The table looked like children's furniture, with him perched atop it, but he ate prodigiously and drank enough beer that Valentinian would have probably slept for three days, had he tried to match the man.

But alone. That was the key to this scam. One other place to check, just to confirm, and Valentinian would head back to the ship.

[20]

KYRIAKI

KYRIAKI HAD NEVER REALLY HAD friends. Not like most people thought of the concept. She had always been too busy trying to out-work, out-study, or out-do the other students to stop and *have friends*. Or anything else. A few semi-drunken, teenage tumbles, when she had consumed enough to overcome her own reservations and try to enjoy herself, but the boys hadn't been any more experienced, and had not impressed her.

After graduation and into work, it had been the same. Twelve- or fourteen- hour days had been common. When others might call it a day after ten and go have a beer, she was doing paperwork or studying. Once or twice she had let co-workers set her up on blind dates, or gone out with someone who had worked up the nerve, but none of them had lit a fire in her.

Later, the White Hats were almost a monastic order unto themselves, which had actually suited her

150

mind even better. There was no pressure to get familiar with her cohorts. To drink with them. To date or become romantically, or even physically involved.

So she was still trying to figure out how to be friends with Bayjy. She was attempting, in her own, awkward way, to break out of the shell she had engulfed herself in. She would ask questions and then try to understand the answers, with so little cultural context. Everyone had seen or done so much more than her.

But she was trying.

And Bayjy seemed to understand. The mauve woman wasn't physically holding her hand, but perhaps metaphorically. Since Valentinian had forbid the woman from leaving the ship, Kyriaki had volunteered to shop for her. She had a list and preferred colors.

Bayjy, under that gray outermost layer, was a riot of colors, which Kyriaki had never even suspected. The face Bayjy showed to the universe was so quiet. Like someone else Kyriaki knew. Maybe that's why she was helping.

So she had a list as she found a store that seemed to specialize in apparel for women, rather than women spacers. As Kyriaki had surmised, females in space tended to dress in whatever clothing best fit from the men's section, if only because that was the only way to get sufficient pockets.

Bayjy wanted truly girlie stuff.

Boy-shorts as lacy, racy, and bright as Kyriaki could find. T-shirts with the rudest sayings and images they might sell. Socks with kitties or dragons on them. Bayjy had managed to purchase a couple of bras after her old Captain had abandoned her, so Kyriaki didn't have to try to find a match there. And Kyriaki had almost suggested the woman go without, like she herself did, but that might be a step too far for Bayjy right now.

This place seemed to fit the bill, as she entered.

Kyriaki found the bin where panties were displayed. She pulled out her card-reader and snapped a picture, sending it over the line as she called Bayjy.

"What about this?" Kyriaki asked as the woman answered.

"Can you send me a picture of that bright blue pair down a shelf and to the left in the picture," Bayjy's grin was infectious, even over the comm.

Kyriaki pulled them flat and sent the next picture.

"Oh, yeah. Gimme," Bayjy said. "Two pairs in blue and one of the yellow, if it's the right size."

"Done," Kyriaki grabbed her prizes and began to move around.

She had picked this store because they also had a machine that would print images on shirts for a fee.

"Here," Kyriaki said, stepping back to snap the whole wall and transmit it.

"What are you doing?" a woman appeared from somewhere with a cross look on her face. "No pictures of my stock."

"My friend got in trouble with the Captain," Kyriaki put her most charming self on. "No shore leave on this trip, so I volunteered to shop for her. Need to send her pictures so she can see what she wants me to buy."

"Seriously?" the cranky old woman asked.

"Hang on," Kyriaki said to everyone. "Bayjy, putting you on speaker."

"Okay, second row from the top, number five from the left in the picture," Bayjy said, suddenly standing next to her, however virtually. "Is that a beer company logo?"

"Whiskey," the old woman said, loud enough for the card-reader to pick it up.

"Awesome," Bayjy laughed. "Gimme one in Vermillion and one in Magenta, three quarter sleeves."

"You want three quarters or raglan?" Kyriaki asked, snapping a picture of the shirt styles on the right and sending.

"Ooh, one of each. You pick, Kyriaki," Bayjy sounded like an eight-year-old in a candy store now. "Do they have silks? Mine are getting old."

"Silks?" the woman merchant asked.

"Thermal base layer," Kyriaki said. "My friend is Pranai, so she needs lots of warm clothes, most of the time."

"Just that," the shopkeeper grumbled and pointed.

Kyriaki followed her finger and found a jumbled bin of what looked like either leftovers, or stuff to buy if you were going mountain climbing on the surface of a hostile, cold planet. Gray, gray, gray.

"Oh, hey, here you go," Kyriaki sent a snap. "You'll have to cut them off to fit, or double the wrists and ankles, but baby blue?"

"Mine," Bayjy said after a moment to look at the latest image.

Behind her, Kyriaki could hear the printer machine warming up, so she headed back, pausing to locate two shirts for her friend from a stack of open-faced cubes. Not quite magenta, but loud enough. And the raglan was white on the torso and the brightest vermillion red arms she could remember.

Socks were by the counter as she approached. After she handed the shopkeeper the shirts, Kyriaki started rifling.

"Okay, got socks," she announced, grabbing two packages.

"What are they?" Bayjy asked. "Picture's not coming through."

"It's a surprise," Kyriaki laughed. "Got you taken care of. Now I need some stuff for me. See you in a bit."

"Love you much," Bayjy blew a kiss across the line.

Kyriaki blushed. She smiled at the pair of them both thrust into whole new universes.

Trusting others.

Kyriaki's entire wardrobe was functional and whatever the opposite of eye-catching was. Demure, maybe? Crocodile-green pants. Gray or black shirts. Gray kangaroo overshirt.

Bayjy only appeared to be the same on the surface, because all the colorful silliness was hidden from the casual stranger.

Since she was done picking things out for Bayjy, Kyriaki went and picked herself out some of the brightest pink panties the shop had. And a package of red ones with white hearts on them. Every pair she had ever owned to date had either been white or gray, including the ones she had on.

Maybe Bayjy was on to something. Kyriaki could still look formal and demure, while hiding a secret underneath. She was, but now she could have several.

Maybe this was what it was like to become a pirate?

[21]

VALENTINIAN

VALENTINIAN GRINNED as he confirmed it, but hadn't been surprised. Dave, of all people, had taught him the trick. When you docked with a station, you always had to file papers with the authorities listing all your crew, even those who weren't going to need to go aboard the station anyway.

Mostly it was a formality for law enforcement, in case somebody had a warrant listed. Or leftover fines to pay, like he had faced back at Bohrne. The information wasn't generally public, but this was like Laurentia. As Dave had shown, you could pay a small fee and get the information as a secondary feed, if you really wanted it.

Butler Vidy-Wooders, Captain of *Hard Bargain*, hadn't listed any crew. Not necessarily an impossible situation, but uncommon enough. Most ships had two aboard, if only because sometimes you might get into trouble and need a spare set of hands in an emergency. He had always had a first mate for that reason.

And *Hard Bargain* was nearly three times the size of *Longshot Hypothesis*, in overall volume, but Bayjy had said that most of the forward two-thirds of the ship was cargo hold, with a small pilothouse sticking out of the top deck to help maneuver when you got close to your wreck. It barely had more crew quarters than Valentinian's ship, but the *Longshot* was a dedicated fast cargo runner with passenger capacity, not a salvager.

Hard Bargain was engines and crew space, with enough empty volume to haul whatever you might find, either to a station, or to the ground.

But it had also only been about twelve weeks since the man had abandoned his crew, presumably as a factor of his greed. Or maybe he was just an asshole.

There was always that.

There wasn't much Valentinian could do about Bayjy's share of the payout, but there were still things they could do about the captain.

He was back at his rear airlock hatch waiting for it to cycle completely open so he could board. This wasn't a day he was expecting anyone to come running down the concourse at him with an arrest warrant, so he was relaxed.

Dave met him in the airlock and made sure it was him. They went forward to find Kyriaki and Bayjy waiting in the rec room. Valentinian paused long enough to grab a glass of juice from the pitcher in this refrigerator and then settled. He wasn't used to keeping parts of the ship warmer, but every little bit helped Bayjy function, and he could sweat a little. At least for now.

"And?" Bayjy was practically vibrating with mad energy. Even worse than normal for her.

"He has not replaced his crew, as of yet," Valentinian nodded. "Might be recruiting here, but I can't tell until he files the official paperwork, and he has not."

"So it might work?" Kyriaki completed the thought.

"Unless he is hiding stowaways on his ship, which is all sorts of fines and problems," Valentinian said. "You should have space to work. Too bad we're not docked closer, but this was the hand they dealt us. Questions?"

"You know he's a damned good player, right?" Bayjy's voice mixed sternness and concern in equal parts.

"Yes, ma'am," Valentinian grinned back. "Not that bad of a slouch myself, you know."

"Well, yes," Bayjy allowed. "I seem to remember a crooked game you came out smelling like roses from."

"That's his specialty, Bayjy," Dave laughed. "That's why I picked the man. It's why Kyriaki had such a hard time sorting everything out when she was chasing me. It's his super-power."

Valentinian was unused to blushing, so it felt utterly alien, especially when the others laughed all the harder at his discomfort. But there was a truth to the big man's words. Smelling like a rose was his thing.

"Okay," Valentinian finally brought things back to seriousness. "We'll assume he keeps something of a regular schedule, since Bayjy says he was always a creature of habit before. We'll be up early in the morning so they can swing by and take most of the cargo off, then nap in the afternoon and prepare for the show later."

"Most of the cargo?" Bayjy asked.

"I'm kind of enjoying pineapple juice and coconut milk," Valentinian said. "Add some soda water and it's a nice, refreshing drink. I seem to be sweating more than I used to, so fluid intake is important and will continue to be."

And apparently a Pranai could blush as well. Or something. Her skin turned a darker shade rushing down towards indigo for a few moments.

"Thank you," she said finally, addressing all the implications that he was keeping her as part of the crew later, which had not been a foregone conclusion.

"We still have to pull this off and get away," he replied.

His part was easy enough, as he was the bright shiny distraction on this one. The other three would have to work together. He knew Dave and Kyriaki had done that sort of thing before, but Bayjy was going to have to step up and be more than just a Senior Cutter now.

[22]
VALENTINIAN

VALENTINIAN LOOKED at his empty cargo bay and held a quiet sigh inside. For better than two years, he had made an honest-enough living running cargos around the Dominion as people needed things *now*. But for Dave, he'd have been looking at the same sort of mundane adventures for the next twenty years, which had not particularly filled him with angst.

But with the crates of fruit gone, a small portion of his life had gone with them. Success in the cargo industry meant reliability and trust. Being on something of a set schedule, running between certain stars often enough that merchants and shippers would come to rely on being able to hire you to do things.

Even Solaria Femina hadn't really interrupted that, at least initially, because he could have continued to transport small things, as long as they were on Madame Cleray's itinerary. Since that was published, merchants would have known definitively when they could hire him and where he was headed.

But he had just offloaded possibly his last ever legitimate cargo from the bay of *Longshot Hypothesis*. Future jobs would be up to him, buying low and trying to find a place to sell high, while avoiding pirates and the Widow and trying to make his margins.

Salvaging wasn't his first choice, but being a wanted fugitive did have a tendency to limit your options.

Valentinian sighed, out loud this time, and turned around to find Kyriaki standing silently in the hatchway to the engineering spaces.

"You okay?" she asked.

Valentinian shrugged.

"Pretty sure I'm too young to have had this many careers cut short by circumstances," he replied, not moving towards her, even though he had been planning to have a quick nap followed by a big, late lunch. "Just gotta land on my feet again."

"You are good at it, you know?" she offered.

Again, he shrugged, unwilling to put it into words. She had also given up her career on one hell of a hand of cards. Valentinian wasn't sure why she hadn't killed him and Dave at some point, and really wasn't sure he wanted to dig deeper into the woman's psyche.

Understanding a woman's motives had never been his strong suit. Even simple women, which was not a term he would ever use to describe Kyriaki Apokapes. Or Bayjy Endon.

"Yeah, I suppose," Valentinian agreed, more or less. "But up until now, I was mostly on the law-abiding side of the line. From here on in, we don't have that option. And if this works and we're out into Wildspace after that, there is no law, except what we take with us, from what I've heard. That changes a lot of equations."

"Regretting your collection of lost geese?" she asked. This time, she stepped one pace forward. Not into his space, but reducing the amount of gap between them.

"No, actually," Valentinian felt his face brighten up. "That's one part I wouldn't change. And I wouldn't want to know the kind of captain who did make those sorts of choices."

"Even me?" she asked, somehow another step closer yet. It was like the tides of a black hole, invisibly tugging them towards an event horizon.

"Especially you, Kyriaki," he found himself saying in a quieter voice that better suited being only a meter away from her, instead of the longer distance when they had started talking. "You could have taken Dave or I down any number of times, had you wanted to. I'm sorry you had to give up everything, when the ethics of the situation got crossways with the law, but that's kind of where I live."

He could have touched her now. Reached out a hand and rested it on her arm. She could have done the same, and both of them were studiously not doing that, even though soon they might be dancing at this rate.

"So now what?" she asked, quiet.

"Tonight, we try to pay the captain of the *Hard Bargain* back in some measure for his shitty behavior," Valentinian felt his face grow hard. "Then probably run like hell again tomorrow. And we keep running, until either the Widow gives up, or we are so far away that nobody out there has even heard of the Dominion. At some point, I presume we'll all need new identities, issued wherever we end up, either out in Wildspace or beyond."

"So you expect we'll stay together as a crew?" her voice had something else in it now.

Hope? Hard to tell. She always played her cards close to the vest.

"Until I have a reason not to," he answered.

They hung, frozen in space like a binary system, two stars orbiting a common point in close proximity, unwilling to move any closer or further apart.

"I hope I'm not interrupting?" Dave suddenly called out.

Valentinian saw Kyriaki blushing almost as hard as he felt himself doing, as they both turned to face the hatch, still carefully not touching.

Dave had a mean grin on his face, which suddenly morphed into utter innocence.

"So, you've always told me that when one of the feed line markers goes yellow to come grab you, at least until you're confident I'm ready to take part of the engine apart," Dave drawled in an off-hand manner. "So starboard secondary went dark yellow in the last day or so. Figure we should fix it now, since we might have to pull a Bohrne getaway later. You got some free time, Vee?"

Valentinian wasn't sure if he wanted to thank the man for the interruption, or punch him. Maybe both. But at least the mad current of energy between he and Kyriaki had been broken, before he did something he lived to regret. Or worse, didn't regret.

He nodded to the woman and listened to her own breathing trying to ratchet down to merely normal.

"Now'd be better, Dave," Valentinian said,

moving forward to where the big guy was carrying the toolkit easily in one hand. "Then some food and all the adventures."

He paused as Dave started forward, turning just enough to look at Kyriaki. She was blushing, but smiled at the little secret they shared. Maybe not so little, since Dave had probably been standing there watching for a while before he said something.

But yeah, now was not the time to get entangled with that woman. At least any more than he already was.

[23]

DAVE

HE HAD NEVER REALLY BEEN a poker player, but Dave already knew he didn't have the temperament for it. Poker was a game of subtlety and guile, generally with strangers. Living inside the bubble of the Dominion Household, there hadn't been any strangers. Ever.

As a result, he had gravitated towards all manner of board game combat simulations instead, from full electronic fleet maneuver games down to squad-level, tactical stuff with inch-tall, hand-painted miniatures. Things that kept a warrior like the Dominator sharp.

Vee was an exceptional poker player. That much was obvious, both from the records of the man and from Dave's personal experience. Even the crooked game on Bohrne had shown how well the man could adjust things to his preference.

Dave had listened to Valentinian explain it all, and followed maybe a third of the details. But he didn't need to really understand, as he wasn't about to start playing with card sharps like you found on a space station. At least until he found someone playing *Support Squad War Patrol* on a one-by-two table. Then he might break out the old skills.

But it was amazing to watch Vee set somebody up.

Dave had gone in early, finding a spot on one end of the bar and getting a burger. Vee had wandered in later, grabbing a mug of beer and setting himself up at a table in the corner that seemed, of common consent, to be dedicated to card games on just about every station.

Maybe the poker players had trained everyone else to drink elsewhere?

Valentinian had settled down, sipping his beer and pulling out a deck of Arcades cards. He was quickly playing some local version of solitaire, but hadn't gone more than three minutes when another player wandered over to watch. And then a third.

Seriously, was Vee broadcasting pheromones or something? Putting out a hypersonic call that only card players could hear? A fourth arrived about the time Valentinian had shuffled all the cards back together, his solitaire forgotten.

Dave was reminded of making rock candy with his daughter, when she was about six. Nothing but watching, and then magic happened. Bang, you had a card game.

"Gentlemen," Valentinian acknowledged the men in a friendly drawl. "Did you have the table reserved?"

"No," one of them spoke up. "Was wondering

about perhaps playing some Arcades in a low-buy, table-stakes kind of game."

Dave processed the words. Low-buy meant small bids and a small game. Table stakes meant you put your cash on the table at the beginning, and stayed with it. If you lost that, you were out, unless the rest of the players decided to let you buy back in, but any of them could veto such a move.

It was, as much as a group of strangers met in a bar could assemble, a friendly, neutral game. Killing time amiably, as Vee had explained it, rather than cutting out a mark and fleecing him for everything he was worth, like had happened on Bohrne. Or when Vee first got the funds to buy the *Longshot Hypothesis*.

A way to pass the evening, on a cold night on the ranch with some friends.

Dave shrugged internally as he watched, learning a whole other side of human nature in the process.

In his head, he was watching the clock. He had always been able to tell time internally to a withering degree of accuracy. The Caelons frequently used such measures in missions and raids, and required every trooper do it without assistance.

Butler Vidy-Wooders came into the bar less than a minute early, according to the schedule Valentinian had built for everyone. The four players in the corner were only just pulling up chairs and ordering drinks when the M'Rai captain walked over, a keen smile on his face.

"Were you gentlemen about to set up a game?" the giant asked in a companionable voice.

"Just getting to that point, sir," Valentinian said in a quiet, careful tone. "Hadn't even agreed to our table stakes, yet, but the consensus is a low-buy game. At least at first. Haven't played with any of the others here, so I don't know how long it might go, or what their comfort level is. Gentlemen?"

Dave was amazed at how Valentinian played a group of men who had a decade or three on him. Dangle the bait out there like he was the mark, to use the term Vee had taught him. Watch the others circle like curious sharks.

"One thousand Union Krodageni?" one of the men suggested.

He had the look to Dave of a semi-successful merchant. It was in his clothing and carriage. Forty, perhaps. Not fabulously wealthy, but successful enough, at least for this sector, to play poker in a bar with strangers for a reasonable amount of money.

The others hemmed and hawed for a bit. One thousand was at the high end for friendly poker, especially with five players, but it also would make the game more interesting.

And that was a pot that seemed to draw Vidy-Wooders in like flame led a moth. He quickly pulled up a spot and ended up more or less across from Valentinian. The merchant was between them on Vee's right, and two other men who looked like spacers or low-end captains ended up on Valentinian's left.

The layout reminded Dave of the game where the Sheriff had set the loud boy up to be swept.

They could have played with Valentinian's deck, but courtesy called for them to use a clean one, so Vee dropped the three Union Krodageni to have a new box delivered instead, still wrapped in plastic film. Nobody could mark them easily, that way.

An honest, wholesome way to spend an evening.

Dave smiled and pulled out his card-reader, sending a message to Kyriaki as the first ante went round the table and the first cards were dealt.

TECHNICALLY, she *was* the expert, but that just meant she had done this once before. Kyriaki wasn't sure that the other woman with her didn't have far more experience sneaking into dark, quiet starships, but Bayjy had never had to work on the possibility of live defenders suddenly appearing and opening fire. Just booby-traps and faulty reactors acting up.

Kyriaki didn't figure that the captain of *Hard Bargain* would leave bombs on his ship, but her raid onto *Longshot Hypothesis* had been planned by the Widow for a lethal encounter. She had carried detonators and a flamer on that mission, rather than stun grenades and a shock pistol.

Bayjy had said she had never shot anyone in her life. So maybe that did make Kyriaki the expert.

She had shot a number of people over the years. And she was pretty sure most of them had deserved it.

So they were up tight to the outside of the station, moving like ghosts on the outer skin, with radios turned to the lowest transmitting power and magnetic boots holding them in place, just waiting.

Dave's message came through as a text on the Heads Up Display in her spacesuit. She had borrowed this one, and it was a clumsy fit, even with everything pulled in with straps. Artaxerxes had been only a little taller, but so much larger around the middle.

Poker game begun, it read.

Kyriaki reached out a hand and gave Bayjy a thumbs up signal. They had time, hopefully, to be methodical. That was Bayjy's expertise, getting around antique security systems to steal treasure.

Hard Bargain wasn't an antique, but Bayjy had spent the better part of three years aboard, before this, so she hopefully knew all the tricks necessary to get in. If Vidy-Wooders was playing poker, they had time, assuming they didn't set off an alarm.

And Dave would be able to warn them, hopefully.

Bayjy led her forward, towards the bow of *Hard Bargain*, docked snugly on the cargo deck. The higher deck on the station was where passenger transports would load, and it had wide portholes for people to watch ships come and go. Down here the walls were flat steel plates with cargo transports stuck out from them like thumbs.

Like *Longshot Hypothesis*, *Hard Bargain* had airlocks at either end. The big one where cargo came and went, plus a small personnel airlock, were nose in. They walked quickly up the side of the salvage vessel to get to the port access lock. Kyriaki had her fingers mentally crossed that nobody would happen by in a station-flitter and see them. Or if they did, the watcher would assume they were doing external maintenance.

The alternative would be a quick call to station security to have them arrested for burglary. Which would cost them their only chance to do this to the man short of an armed confrontation later.

This airlock looked unused as she and Bayjy approached it, just like Valentinian's forward lock had been. Most people went in and out on a station while docked, so they tended to use the same paths on the surface of a planet as well. Muscle memory.

Hard Bargain was also a perfectly weird layout for a ship. Both ends of the big cargo bay forward had oversized airlocks. When the crew was working, they left the entire bay in vacuum for weeks on end, only closing up and pressurizing when they were ready to leave. As a result, the crew had the habit of going in and out through the cargo bay hammered into them, because that was where the valuables and tools were.

Kyriaki moved to one side and turned to watch as much sky as she could while Bayjy worked. The silence would probably eat at most people. Kyriaki had frequently gone days without saying a word, especially if she was on a case.

Silence was her friend.

Bayjy worked. Kyriaki watched. Time passed.

Bayjy turning got Kyriaki's attention. Thumbs up.

Hopefully, she had disabled the outermost layer of security. And hopefully, Vidy-Wooders wasn't as paranoid as Valentinian had been, and so hadn't built an entire second system that wasn't connected to the first one. Any other vessel, any other captain, and Kyriaki would have had to face the hard decision of shooting those two men, because she could have snuck up close enough, probably.

She was pleased that they were friends now. Maybe she'd survive.

Kyriaki typed out a quick message to Dave from the keyboard on her left forearm.

Stage one complete.

Dave knew what that meant. Nobody else would.

Kyriaki returned the thumbs up to Bayjy and watched the woman push a big, green button on the keyboard. Internally, the airlock would make sure the inner door was sealed, and then evacuate all the air and prepare to open the outer door to a pair of cat burglars in matching vermillion T-shirts. With whiskey logos between their breasts.

And if it set off an alarm, Dave would see the man who owned the ship do something. Maybe he'd suddenly run away from the game. Maybe he would call station security.

They were on shaky legal ground if they got arrested, but not completely lost. Kyriaki was all set to make a case to a magistrate that they were just reclaiming Bayjy's gear. Then Vidy-Wooders would have to explain to a court what he had done to his previous crew, after which his name wouldn't be worth warm spit to competent spacers anywhere.

You think cops are clannish and unforgiving? Piss off spacers in a public way by mistreating them, Butler.

Finally, the outer hatch opened. Kyriaki watched her screen, but no emergency abort messages came through. She let go the tense breath she had been holding as Bayjy watched, and then moved.

Inside, the airlock was in poor shape. Like it hadn't been cleaned in years. And it needed it.

Grease from something had oozed down a wall and then crystalized into a layer of armor over the gray steel. Two suits were on racks, but both had been cannibalized for spare parts at some point, with someone, somewhere needing both right arms, plus a left hand and a right boot.

Must have been one hell of a party.

Bayjy worked while Kyriaki managed communications security.

Nothing. Hopefully, that meant no alarm, instead of an automated system that notified the station rather than the captain.

Vidy-Wooders, from Bayjy's stories, didn't strike Kyriaki as the type to rely on unknown Stationmasters doing their jobs for him.

The outer hatch closed. The system began to pressurize with flashing lights and slowly-growing sound as the vacuum abated.

Still, no alarms.

Now the fun part.

Bayjy unlocked her faceplate and opened it, so Kyriaki joined her. No radios unless necessary.

"Ready?" the mauve woman asked.

Kyriaki drew a heavy stun pistol and pointed it at the inner hatch.

"Go," she said.

They were sort of trapped right now, if the inner hatch had an alarm on it. It would require precious minutes to cycle the airlock such that they could escape back into vacuum, if something went wrong at this point.

[25]
VALENTINIAN

ARCADES IS A GAME OF CHANCE, mixed with skill and luck.

That had been the first lesson Valentinian's dad had taught him, when he sat his young son down to teach him the game.

Nikephoros Tarasicodissa had started a family late, already in his fifties and largely ready to settle down. Valentinian's disgrace had ricocheted back and pretty much pushed Nikephoros into permanent retirement from the tentative state he had occupied before.

But he had taught his son how spacers killed time between runs and while alone in the isolation of a warpbubble.

Turned out Valentinian was pretty good at it.

Most of a card game like Arcades poker was learning the unconscious fidgets another player telegraphs when the cards are good or bad. When he's bluffing or when he's sandbagging you. Professionals learn to suppress them entirely, and then offer up false signals that make suckers out of amateurs.

The man on Valentinian's left, the one who looked like a middle-aged captain, was a pro. The merchant on his right was a studied amateur. The other spacer with them was a mark.

Butler Vidy-Wooders was a card sharp. And a bully, but Valentinian knew that already.

A man who had been bigger than anyone but immediate family while still a kid, and grew into a monster who could push anyone around as an adult.

Of course, the shock pistol on Valentinian's right thigh today was a different model than he normally carried. For some reason, he'd gone into the armory and pulled out the heaviest version he had and strapped it on. It might kill the average human, if he had to shoot someone, even in self-defense.

It would work just fine on a M'Rai bodybuilder with a chip on his shoulder.

Hopefully tonight was just a long con, a shell game where things weren't what they appeared.

Valentinian really didn't care if he ended up losing the table stakes he had put down. Right now, he was still playing with profits from that punk back on Bohrne.

Twenty minutes in, and the mark was toast. It was almost a blessing to the man to wipe him out quickly and let him sit back to watch. Maybe he would learn a few things about the game from expert players.

Valentinian and Vidy-Wooders had pretty much split the mark's funds between them, with the other two running about even from where they had started.

With an honest deck, people get lucky, and this

early in the night, nobody was betting huge amounts to try to force hands and pots.

Mostly a friendly thing. Without the M'Rai glowering at people, it might have even been a pleasant evening with strangers. Many poker games turned out that way, if nobody had an axe to grind.

The deal was back to Valentinian. He shuffled the cards a little sloppy, just because he could, and kicked a chip into the pot for an ante. Arcades was a game of seven cards. He dealt everyone one card up, one down, and one up, nodding to the man on his right to bid, sitting on an unmatched pair of Wedgestones, one granite and one bronze.

A *Perfect Arcade* had six cards, all in one suit: Capstone, both Wedgestones, both Columns, and the Threshold. If you built from more than one suit, you had a *Mixed Arcade*. Without a Capstone, you had a *Hallway*, for the third best hand you could Build. With everything but a Threshold, you had a *Tunnel*.

It went down from there, with a *Corridor* being just Wedgestones and Columns, and then you got into Patterns of Six of a Kind, down to Four. It could be a complicated game to learn all the ways winning hands balanced against each other, but mostly it was a game of people.

Watching them. Learning how their mind worked from the way the eyes dilated. It would have been most fun to have Sheriff Bolat-Nurlan here at the table tonight. But that man was a storyteller with a violin for a voice. Take you up or down, as the story unfolded.

"Two," the merchant bid, kicking in a pair of chips to the pot.

It was early in the hand. Nobody was going to go

all in at this point. Certainly not on three of seven cards. The best hand you could have right now would be matching up a Capstone with both Wedgestones. And that only gave you a High Stack. Four of a kind could beat that, and wasn't hard to draw when there were twelve Columns or Wedgestones in the deck.

So Valentinian was a little surprised when Butler raised on the first round.

"Five," the M'Rai bully said with a semi-triumphant growl and a disdainful flick to toss the chips into the pot.

The two cards up were a Wedgestone and a Threshold, so he was already bluffing, pushing people to expect an Arcade later.

Valentinian held his internal commentary tight and let his face show a curious disbelief. That sort of thing had worked well with the punk. It tended to work well with players who substituted intimidation for skill.

He had three Columns. Possibly he could build an Arcade, depending on how the cards went, but still a winning hand by itself, one time in five.

The other players called and play continued.

Valentinian smiled and dealt. He didn't have to beat the man at the table. His was just the pretty face that distracted you while the bad people went to work in the shadows.

[26]

BAYJY

THE DAMNED SHIP hadn't changed one iota since she left. Didn't even look like Butler had bothered to clean anything, from the thin smear of dust starting to settle.

Bayjy let herself growl as she looked around the kitchen area.

"Problem?" Kyriaki asked from close by.

That chick hadn't put her gun down since they boarded, and held it in a way that told Bayjy she'd shot people before. Maybe a lot of them. Plus Dave had taken Bayjy aside yesterday and given her the complete low-down on everything that had happened on a planet named Tartarus. So Kyriaki was trouble cubed.

At least the cop was on her side.

"No," Bayjy replied. "Offended at bad housekeeping. We kept this place spotless. Butler's a slob."

She moved to the refrigerator and opened it, but that was mostly to confirm the obvious.

All the fresh fruit was gone, as well as the salad fixings they used to grow in the hydroponics bay. Only things in there were one liter beer bottles now. The freezer held nothing but frozen meals in huge trays, enough calories for an angry M'Rai male.

"That's it?" Kyriaki asked, standing next to her.

Bayjy grinned. You could bond with people over the silliest things, like a bachelor's idea of good nutrition.

"That's it," Bayjy agreed. "Wanted to make sure Butler really was the only person aboard. You can hide lots of things, but all the evidence will be in the refrigerator."

"Good to know," her tiny brunette partner nodded. "Now what?"

Bayjy let herself scowl at the room where she and the gang had had such good times. All the birthdays and card games. The lies, the drinking, and the occasional tumble in a bunk after a good run.

All gone.

She'd been the last one left at Bohrne Station, after the others gambled on other ships, other jobs, so Bayjy didn't figure she'd ever see the other six of her friends again, unless she got really lucky with Valentinian, or she went looking.

They were nice enough folks, but nobody she was pining after.

"Personal quarters," Bayjy said aloud, letting her mind wander.

Lucky for them, Butler had been too lazy to close up any of the interior frame bulkheads, so she didn't have to spoof any more of his security.

Being a Cutter meant that you had to know

security systems, both physical and electronic, so you could get into wrecks without having to blast them apart first. Not a skill she had expected to make her a living, back when she was a squirt, but good enough today to help her with revenge.

Crew deck.

Technically, all of this was crew deck, since Butler's suite and the bridge were up a level by themselves, but everyone always referred to this hallway as the crew deck. All their personal cabins were here.

Had been here.

She decided to skip any of the others for now. It would just make her angry, seeing their stuff left as they had put it when they walked away. Her cabin was going to hurt enough that she should stay away from power systems and the engines, at least until she was calm enough to not sabotage them.

"Here," Bayjy said, facing the hatch.

"You okay?" Kyriaki was suddenly standing right next to her, almost offering a shoulder to cry on.

"Angry," Bayjy sighed.

"If this doesn't work, I'll help you shoot him instead," the cop offered with an evil grin.

"Thanks."

Bayjy reached up and keyed her personal code into the door, just on the off-chance that Butler had been too lazy to change them all when he dumped his crew and ran.

The hatch opened. She muttered a particularly colorful curse and thought about finding a voodoo doll of her old captain that she could stick pins into when she felt bad.

Inside, the room was spotless. Impersonal. All of her shit was gone. Her fist impacted the sidewall away from Kyriaki before she realized what she was doing.

That girl's pistol was up and her head was on a swivel as she pivoted and prepared to kill everything that moved.

"Sorry," Bayjy offered. "Overreacted."

"Oh," Kyriaki nodded and rose back up to her full, short height, half a head below Bayjy or the captain. "Room looks cleaner than your cabin on *Longshot Hypothesis*."

For some reason, that broke the band of ice starting to wrap around her chest. Bayjy laughed. Not quite hysterically, but all the pent-up pressures of suddenly being abandoned bubbled up briefly, overflowed, and then receded.

She found herself being held by Kyriaki with no memory of how she got there, when her mind settled back down.

"Thank you," Bayjy wiped her nose and sucked a huge breath into her lungs to purify everything.

"So maybe he packed it all up and stowed it somewhere?" Kyriaki asked. "If he had a major sale coming up, he might want the rest of the shop looking presentable. Plus, you never dump gear you might need later, especially if you have to recruit a new crew tomorrow."

"What would he tell the new people?" Bayjy felt her brow furrow. Bad, that. Good way to get wrinkles. Shouldn't do that in the future.

"Oh, major accident, maybe," Kyriaki shrugged. "Explosion killed everyone over there and he only survived by being here. Without witnesses, anything might be plausible. Where would he put boxes?"

"Primary bay," Bayjy decided. She looked around the room that had been her home for so long and growled.

Forward now, out of the aft end of the ship to the big airlock in the main corridor. This hatch slid sideways into both walls, revealing the huge room where the whole crew could suit up at once, ten meters on a side.

A rainbow on the left caught her eye, and her mind. Bayjy found herself with her arms wrapped around her old heatsuit, crying.

Seriously, she needed to stop that. But this was her heatsuit. Done in ten centimeter, horizontal stripes from ankle to neck. A rainbow in space. 'Cause that was how she rolled.

"Is that…?" Kyriaki had snuck up on her again.

"Yeah," Bayjy grinned.

"So why weren't you wearing it at Bohrne?" the woman asked.

"Because I was going shopping for clothes," Bayjy laughed. "And this thing is a pain in the ass to get on and off in a changing room. And too damned expensive to buy a second one when I was looking at starving."

Gods, she could be warm again. Put it on like a second skin and turn the heat up to the point she could get by with just cute pants and a tight T-shirt to show off her amazing ass and muscles, if she had a knit cap on her bald skull. No more stupid layers and constantly freezing her butt off anyway.

And rainbow stripes when she walked.

"Here," Kyriaki said, digging an oversized bag out of a nearby bin.

In it went.

If Butler still had her heatsuit, he probably had the rest of her gear somewhere close by, too lazy or cheap to get rid of it yet.

And Bayjy knew hope.

DAVE WAS DEEPLY concerned that he might actually learn how to play Arcades at some point, if he kept this up. Leaned against the bar, sipping slowly at the cheapest, thinnest beer they sold. Watching.

It was obvious that the gray giant considered himself a better player than he really was, but most of the rest of the table were probably only as good, if that.

Not counting Valentinian.

Dave watched his captain put on a show, but one that almost everyone would miss, unless they knew what to look for. Or had watched him do it before.

The first man out hadn't been that good. The other two were better, but both were down to perhaps half the money they had started with at this point, winning maybe one hand each to three or four that Vee and Vidy-Wooders took.

Interestingly, Valentinian wasn't betting heavy on good hands, although he would back out and fold on bad ones. Just enough to keep everyone playing.

But Valentinian wasn't trying to clean everyone out. He was providing hours of entertainment while the women did their job and Dave acted as a lifeguard.

Hopefully, the gray giant would sit here all night, and then go back to his ship, no wiser. If an alarm suddenly went off and the man fled, Dave's job would be to either distract him somehow, or attack him.

Anything to give the women time to make their escape, even if Dave ended up spending the night in the drunk tank and had to pay a fine in the morning.

It was hard to judge an opponent who was seated. The man was built like Valentinian, just scaled up fifty percent. Tall and big, reasonably muscled, but not an oversized, muscle-bound bodybuilder who looked like he could tear bulkheads with his bare hands.

Not like Dave.

The man would still be enormously strong, if you got in close. Probably had one hell of a bear hug, if he got you grappled.

But Dave had studied movement under a man who was more than a head shorter than he was, maybe fifty-five kilograms, and approaching eighty years old at the time. Stauracius had had skin like leather and the softest touch of any human Dave had ever met, especially when he got out the acupuncture needles to fix some issue.

Dave had met perhaps three other men in his life who might be as deadly as Stauracius.

Might.

Dave wasn't one of them.

Facing Vidy-Wooders barehanded would be like

wrestling with Stauracius. With him in the role of the weasel, rather than the wolf.

Dave smiled at the ancient memory.

"Ha," Dave heard the M'Rai bark triumphantly as he turned over his cards and started to reach for the pot.

"Just a moment," Valentinian interrupted, turning over his own cards to show a Mixed Arcade that beat the giant's Corridor.

Dave was watching the back of Vidy-Wooders's head, so he could see Vee's face. The man's shoulders flexed in that way they did when you suddenly focused all your energy down into the ground.

Dave poised, shifting his weight forward just enough that he could be on the man's back in two steps if the M'Rai pirate suddenly exploded in violence. The plastic mug of beer wouldn't be a useful weapon, but the liquid inside would blind the man long enough for Dave to hammer soft spots in his back.

The head and neck would be too high to reach effectively, not without drawing his pseudo-sword baton, which he didn't want to do without provocation. However, kidneys would be at shoulder height and nobody's knees were invulnerable unless you had Caelon armor over them.

They were back at Bohrne again. This had been the point where that punk had lost his temper and almost gotten himself shot by the Sheriff. Dave could smell the stink of adrenaline wafting off the M'Rai, along with curses and muttered disbelief that Valentinian had drawn the winning card he needed with his Build.

But he settled. Didn't grab the edge of the table

with both hands and flip it over onto Valentinian as a prelude to a fight. And dueling wasn't legal on this station, so if the big man decided that he wanted an honorable standoff, they would all have to drop down to the surface of the planet first.

Dave wondered how quick Valentinian really was, if it came to a gunfight. Vidy-Wooders had a pistol on his hip, but so did everyone else at the table. And most of the room. The law was thin out here, and the station folks were mostly concerned with keeping a lid on problems.

Not bothering with fights between off-worlders.

The other spacer dropped out of the game now, close enough to broke after the last hand as to not matter. The merchant took the opportunity to do the same, as the emotions were running far higher than normal for what was supposed to be a friendly game of poker by well-met strangers.

Dave wanted to send a message to the other team, but he waited, unwilling to look down right now.

"So, what'll it be, stranger," Vidy-Wooders growled loud enough that the whole bar heard him.

There was enough menace in his voice that Dave was surprised that Valentinian kept both hands on the table. In other places, many men might have reached a hand down and rested it on a pistol. Just in case.

"How about dinner?" Valentinian asked in a neutral voice. "Arcades just isn't nearly as much fun with only two and we've been at it a while. Some steaks might hit the spot."

The giant paused, probably watching to see if he was being mocked, since Vee wasn't cringing at the potential for violence.

"You're a cool one, aren't you?" Vidy-Wooders asked.

Dave watched Valentinian shrug.

The two men were alone at the table now, as the three others had wandered off, with no great showdown imminent.

Dave watched like a hawk. The gray giant would happily take off like a jackrabbit right now, if an alarm sounded on his ship.

"I'm just here killing time," he said so nonchalantly that Dave almost grinned. "Looking for some distractions away from my crew. You?"

"Got no crew," the M'Rai pirate said harshly. "Paid 'em off after the last salvage job because I got tired of all their grousing and whining. Better this way."

"That would be so nice, some days," Valentinian agreed with the man. "Mine are a group of pain-in-the-ass refugees that all probably deserve to be in a jail cells somewhere. Let's have dinner. My treat, since the other three were so happy to provide us funds tonight."

That got an enormous laugh out of the giant.

"I like the way you think, Captain," Vidy-Wooders turned to flag down a waiter with a snap. "Menus."

Dave caught Valentinian's eye as the pirate turned away from Vee. Saw the shell fall away and the cold, hard man he knew emerge, for just a second. It was a message.

Dave turned away from the scene and leaned his weight against the bar. There was a mirror he could use to track issues, but the place was a boring weeknight right now. Money went elsewhere, as did trouble, for the most part, according to Vee's scouting and recon.

He pulled out his card-reader like he was looking something up and sent a quick message.

Ordering dinner now. Game completed friendly.

Hopefully, the women had already found everything they needed.

THE BOXES, stacked up neatly and stashed in an equipment locker along with a number of heavy suits on hangars, reminded Kyriaki of nothing so much as coffins in a mausoleum. Sixty centimeters wide, thirty tall, stacked up with names visible on the ends. Seven of them.

Leftovers from lives abandoned in space without probably so much as a pang. Probably a smirk, from what Bayjy had told her.

The mauve spacer was down on her knees right now, just touching the box with "Endon, B" on the end, middle of the right hand stack.

Kyriaki let Bayjy have a moment to herself. This had to be worse than running away from the White Hats, because at least Kyriaki had agency then. It had been her decision to protect the two men at the cost of her own career.

Bayjy had been abandoned, like a cat left behind in an apartment when the owners moved out abruptly. She was soldiering pretty well, but Kyriaki could tell how fragile the woman was underneath.

That was okay. Kyriaki would take care of her friend. That was in the job description, at least the one she was writing in her head. If Bayjy could teach a hard-ass cop how to not flinch while wearing bright red panties with white hearts on them, then Kyriaki could hold Bayjy's fragile psyche together as she confronted her own past.

"You ready to move things?" Kyriaki asked.

"Yeah," Bayjy's voice was just above a whisper. "I think so."

Kyriaki grabbed the top box and lifted it. Well, slid it forward enough she could get her hands under it and stagger backwards.

"Sorry," Bayjy suddenly rose and held the other half. "He was a pack rat, so I should have mentioned that one would be heavy."

It also didn't help that the narrow box itself was about a meter long, reinforcing the coffin-like ratios in Kyriaki's head.

Together, they rested it to one side and pulled out Bayjy's box. This one was lighter. Opening it, saw mostly clothes, with a few knick-knacks and a reader-slab, an oversized card-reader. Beat to hell, from the looks of it.

Bayjy started crying again as she picked it up.

"This belonged to my grandma," she said between sniffles.

Kyriaki nodded in mute sympathy. She had even less, as most of her gear was either aboard *Dominion-427* in a similar box, or back on Dominion Prime waiting in long-term storage, where she didn't think she would ever get any of it back. Even the space suit she had been wearing when she boarded *Longshot Hypothesis* had been jettisoned into warpspace as a precaution by the boys.

If she had a higher opinion of her looks, Kyriaki might have been tempted to compare that moment to Aphrodite Rising From The Sea, but she knew she was, at most, cute. Not the kind of face that stopped traffic. Maybe the right bottom, in the right circumstances, but you have the butt you deserve, if you're willing to work for it.

"What about the others?" Bayjy asked.

"We'd have to steal a sled," Kyriaki noted. "Worth it?"

"I'd rather we had their lives, than that son of a bitch Butler." Bayjy suddenly stood, putting the reader-slab away with the care afforded a holy relic. "Captain's more likely willing to look for them, later on."

Kyriaki nodded and handed Bayjy the lid.

"I'll pull them out," she said. "Can you find us something that will carry them all? Plus we need your liftersuit, and one for Dave, if there are any big enough."

Bayjy reached out a hand and touched the next suit over on the rack, next to the rainbow one. And then one a few more down. A big one. Maybe big enough.

The mauve spacer turned to her with a serious face.

"That's gonna look like piracy, when someone goes back and reviews video," Bayjy said in a half-hearted attempt to talk herself out of it.

"Tough," Kyriaki snarled. "So we're pirates now. Valentinian will tell you the difference between the legality of the situation, and the ethics. Illegal here is still going to be right."

"Thank you," Bayjy said, scampering off with a sudden skip to her step as Kyriaki watched.

It felt good, being able to do the right thing. Letting Dave, and later Valentinian, escape her on Tartarus had felt that way, however wrong it was in the eyes of the law. Defecting on the deck of his ship, rather than trying to kill the two of them, or disable the ship long enough for the Widow to catch up, had been the right thing.

This was the right thing.

Bayjy was back pretty quickly with a small cargo sled, the kind that had wheels, repulsors, and compressed-air thrusters to maneuver in vacuum. Quickly, they loaded the seven boxes and two armored suits, strapping them down, and moving them up so they could stash the whole unit in the forward airlock.

They found themselves back in the kitchen.

"It's not enough," Kyriaki said out loud.

"What's not?" Bayjy turned to her.

"Just rescuing our prisoners," Kyriaki stated. "There needs to be more. He shouldn't get off so easily. Not with what he did to all of you."

"There's a thin line between juvenile hijinks and destruction of private property," Bayjy said. "Even local authorities would frown on us setting fire to the ship, in spite of us explaining why."

"Noted," Kyriaki said. "Plus, he needs to know you did it, and not just random station thieves breaking in."

"So how would you…"

She broke off there so hard that Kyriaki turned to look the woman full in the face.

The smile on Bayjy's face was a thing of utter beauty.

"What evil just bit you on the ass?" Kyriaki asked, almost cringing to hear. It must be good.

"Well," Bayjy drawled slowly. "If it had to have my signature on it, then we should probably turn the ship's heat up to forty-five or fifty degrees internally. That kind of heat would tell him who was here."

"Yes," Kyriaki agreed with a giggle. "And then disable the controls so he can't turn it back down without first repairing the system."

Just for extra evil, Kyriaki moved to the refrigerator and pulled the door open. She pulled a butter knife from a drawer nearby and wedged it into the hinge, so the door could not close on its own. She did the same with the freezer door.

"Oh, and ruin all the man's food on top of it?" Bayjy asked with a laugh. "I like the way you work, woman."

They shared a laugh and made their way aft to locate the environmental controls.

There was more than one way to get even with a rat bastard like Butler Vidy-Wooders.

THE STEAKS HAD BEEN AMAZING ENOUGH that Valentinian had ended up eating more than half of the kilogram slab of ribeye that had been delivered, and the rest was in a box to haul home for breakfast with the sides. His opponent had eaten it all, plus the potatoes and all the bread, ignoring the fresh vegetables that had been cooked in coconut oil, from the smell.

Valentinian had developed a taste for coconut on Bohrne and in flight here. Maybe he'd have to eat healthier in the future. First, he had to find someone who could keep a hydroponics bay alive, though. And then a place to put one, since he wasn't about to give up his armory. Maybe one of the passenger cabins? He'd have to review schematics.

It was something pleasing to think about, to take Valentinian's mind off his table mate.

Butler Vidy-Wooders was an asshole. No two ways about it. A crude man with bad jokes and food stuck between his teeth because he hadn't brushed them in months. You could do that, if you had them sealed up with enamel, or they were fake. But it gave him horrible breath.

The beard had been trimmed just enough to fit inside a space suit, as had the hair, or he might have gone all in on the Viking look. Valentinian could see him wearing badly-cured animal hides, tromping through a winter forest with an axe in one hand.

Valentinian was enjoying a glass of port, sweet and mellow, while the other man was into his third tankard of dark beer. But none of this was Valentinian's money. And he really didn't care all that much, to see the occasional smile on Dave's face.

Things must be going well, since neither Dave nor the pig had suddenly taken off running for the corridor outside, nor had station security come in to have a quiet chat with everyone about a touchy situation.

His card-reader chirped quietly. The other guy raised an eyebrow and kept chugging his beer noisily, so Valentinian pulled it out and read the note.

Package retrieved. Message delivered.

He had no idea what that meant, but it came from Kyriaki, so they must have been successful. That would make up for having to deal with this asshole for the last four hours.

Not that he expected to never see Butler Vidy-Wooders again. That one would rage fit for the gods when he got back to his ship and eventually sorted out what had happened and who had done it. He would find Bayjy's name listed as part of the crew of *Longshot Hypothesis* and would understand.

It was just a shame that neither he nor Dave could come up with a plausible excuse for shooting the man.

Still, message delivered. That had a pleasant sound to it.

Valentinian rose.

"Trouble?" Vidy-Wooders scoffed. A man with no crew and no troubles in his life.

Just angry ghosts.

"My crew are causing problems," Valentinian said breezily.

As lies went, it was the honest truth, at that. His crew was causing problems, just not for the captain of *Longshot Hypothesis*.

Hard Bargain's captain, on the other hand…

Valentinian nodded to the man.

"Again tomorrow?" he asked.

"Looking forward to it, Captain," Vidy-Wooders growled in an unpleasant, not-quite-threatening way.

Valentinian paid the combined bill, staggering just a little at the price. But it wasn't his money. Three other players, four with the punk on Bohrne, had funded tonight's entertainment.

With his cargo delivered and funds transferred, the next stage could begin.

Valentinian was looking forward to it.

Because right now, he was going to board his ship, file a flight plan, and run like hell for Wildspace.

There was a vessel out there that had been waiting for him for maybe as long as two thousand years, since the Urlan Empire had been destroyed.

If he was lucky, maybe he'd get rich.

Tonight, Valentinian would settle for getting away.

Oh, and for *Message Delivered*.

Blaze Ward writes science fiction in the Alexandria Station universe (Jessica Keller, The Science Officer, The Story Road, etc.) as well as several other science fiction universes, such as Star Dragon, the Collective, and more. He also writes odd bits of high fantasy with swords and orcs. In addition, he is the Editor and Publisher of *Boundary Shock Quarterly Magazine*. You can find out more at his website www.blazeward.com, as well as Facebook, Goodreads, and other places.

Blaze's works are available as ebooks, paper, and audio, and can be found at a variety of online vendors. His newsletter comes out regularly, and you can also follow his blog on his website. He really enjoys interacting with fans, and looks forward to any and all questions—even ones about his books!

Never miss a release!
If you'd like to be notified of new releases, sign up for my newsletter.

I will never spam you or use your email for nefarious purposes. You can also unsubscribe at any time.

http://www.blazeward.com/newsletter/

Connect with Blaze!

Web: www.blazeward.com
Boundary Shock Quarterly (BSQ):
https://www.boundaryshockquarterly.com/

facebook.com/KRPBlaze

goodreads.com/Blaze_Ward

bookbub.com/authors/blaze-ward